THE MINUTE BOYS OF BUNKER HILL

"AND THEN THE BOY WAITED FOR THE NEXT MOVE"

THE MINUTE BOYS OF BUNKER HILL

BY

EDWARD STRATEMEYER

AUTHOR OF

THE MINUTE BOYS OF LEXINGTON,
THE MINUTE BOYS OF THE GREEN MOUNTAINS,
A YOUNG VOLUNTEER IN CUBA,
UNDER DEWEY AT MANILA, ETC.

ILLUSTRATED BY

J. W. KENNEDY

LOST CLASSICS BOOK COMPANY
PUBLISHER
LAKE WALES
FLORIDA

PUBLISHER'S NOTE

Recognizing the need to return to more traditional principles in education, the Lost Classics Book Company is republishing forgotten late 19th and early 20th century literature and textbooks to aid parents in the education of their children.

This edition of *The Minute Boys of Bunker Hill* was reprinted from the 1899 copyright edition. Changes have been made to update archaic spelling and grammar.

———+———

Library of Congress Catalog Card Number: 98-84149
ISBN 1-890623-05-9

Edward Stratemeyer

Edward Stratemeyer, the son of a German immigrant, was born in Elizabeth, New Jersey, on October 4, 1862. After graduation from high school in the 1880s, he began writing juvenile fiction. His first story was published in 1888, and he soon became a regular contributor to several boys' magazines. He then began to write adventure series published under various pen names at a prodigious rate. His rapid success enabled him to found the Stratemeyer Literary Syndicate in New York City in 1906. Hiring a stable of writers, he supplied characters, plot outlines, and pseudonyms for what quickly became the largest juvenile fiction publishing enterprise in the country. Stratemeyer himself wrote an estimated 160 books under his many pseudonyms, perhaps 60 under his own name, and outlined stories for about 800 more, supplying several generations of boys and girls with endless opportunities for harmless fun and adventure. He died in Newark, New Jersey, on May 10, 1930.

Contents

———+———

CONTENTS

List of Illustrations

———+———

THE

MINUTE BOYS OF BUNKER HILL

———+———

CHAPTER I

ROGER DETERMINES TO LEAVE HOME

"I KNOW it is taking a big risk, Mother. But Mr. Winthrop says he wants his cattle, and I don't blame him. In these days twelve good cows are worth some money."

"I agree with you, Roger; but an expedition to Hog and Noddle's Islands may prove very disastrous. Since our awful fight here in Lexington, and at Concord, and down in Charlestown, the British have been in an ugly mood; and if they discover what is going on, they will send a guard over to the islands to kill every minuteman, or take him a prisoner."

"Mr. Winthrop and the others are going to try to get to the islands and back before the British soldiers realize what is going on."

"How many head of cattle are there on the two islands?"

"About five hundred, so Dick said, besides some horses and a good lot of sheep. Now that we have the British penned in Boston, it would be a shame to let them grow fat on the livestock belonging to the colonists. I'd fight them again before I'd give them a single head," and Roger Morse's manly face showed that he meant what he said.

"Oh, my son, don't talk about fighting again!" cried Mrs. Morse, in quick alarm. "Why, that wound in your head isn't healed up yet, and poor Hen is still limping around from the dreadful treatment he received at the hands of those redcoats. Wait, at least, until you are better."

"I'm well enough to take my place among the minute boys. Don't you think so, Dorothy?" and Roger appealed to his sister, who had just entered the sitting room of the Morse homestead with a bowl of gruel for the invalid mother.

"That is for you to say, Roger," was the answer of the girl, who, since the death of her father, had had the care of the household on her shoulders. "But if you go away, and Hen goes, I really don't know what will become of the farm."

"And what will become of the farm if the British break out of Boston, come here again, and start another fight? You may be certain, if they get a chance, they'll burn down every building in sight."

"God forbid that such a thing should happen, my son!" murmured Mrs. Morse. For a moment she sipped her gruel in silence. "Then you'll really think of going?"

"Unless you say I must stay at home, I intend to leave on Friday. The cattle owners are going over to the islands on Saturday, and I would like to be with Mr. Winthrop and Dick."

"What about Hen? Are you going to take him with you?"

"No, I think he ought to stay home a few days or a week longer. The bruise on his knee isn't quite healed up yet."

"I do not see how I am to spare both of you again," sighed Mrs. Morse. "But duty is duty, I know, and our colonies need every man they can get, in order to vindicate our rights. Yet the boys—"

"I've heard Israel Putnam's youngest son is in the Connecticut volunteers. He isn't sixteen yet. If Old Put allows his son to go to the front, why—"

"Then Roger shall go," finished Dorothy Morse, promptly, as she threw her arm over her only brother's shoulder. "But, oh, Roger, do take care of yourself! Remember those redcoats can fire quite as true as our minutemen, and their bullets are just as deadly."

"You can rest assured that I'll be careful," laughed

the youth, much relieved to think that there had not been a "scene" over his intended departure. "But there is one thing that is worrying me. All told, I haven't over a pint of powder around the place."

"Cannot you get more from some of our soldiers?"

"Get more? Why, half a dozen of them have begged me for what I have. They say those around the Neck haven't over ten rounds of ammunition apiece. If General Gage knew that, how he would come out to lay them low! But he doesn't know it, and our officers are taking great precautions so that he shan't find out."

"You'll have to leave some powder for Hen," put in Dorothy. "He wouldn't like it if he was left without any."

"I intend to leave him half. But I've got another scheme in my head," went on Roger, as he began to pace the floor. "You remember that old stone house in the woods, up near Grayley's—the house in which that Sergeant Kegan and his men made me a prisoner? Well, I imagine those fellows left some powder there— in fact, I am half certain of it. I'm going over there this afternoon to have a look, and Paul Darly is going over with me."

"What makes you imagine that they left powder there?" questioned Dorothy, with interest.

"One of the soldiers—a fellow named Windotte— carried a little keg slung in a strap. When they took me into the building, I noticed that he placed the keg out of sight, on the top shelf of the cupboard. I believe he intended to come back for it later on, but since that time I've got to thinking it over, and I don't believe he ever had the chance to go back, for he was badly wounded down by Buckman's Tavern. If the keg had powder in it, and it is still there, it will be a big prize to uncover—just now," concluded the boy.

Roger Morse was a tall, well-built, manly youth of sixteen years, who lived with his mother and his only sister, Dorothy, on the outskirts of Lexington, on a homestead farm, facing the old Boston road. The farm was one of the most productive in the neighborhood, and since the death of his father, some years previous, Roger had taken entire charge of the outside work, assisted in these duties by Hen Peabody, a hired man of all work.

Mrs. Morse was a lady of forty-five, who had been more or less of an invalid for years. She depended almost entirely upon Roger; Dorothy, who was two years older than her brother; and the ever faithful Hen, who had long since been accepted as an additional member of the household. Hen was from the Green Mountain district, a patriot to the core, and a man who thought his young master "jest right, always."

In a previous work, entitled *The Minute Boys of Lexington*, the particulars are related of how, one morning in April, Roger was stopped on the road by a British detachment of soldiers, made a prisoner, and taken to an old stone house, situated in dense woods. From this place, the youth escaped, to learn that the troops at Boston were coming out to Concord and Lexington to confiscate the military stores secreted at those places. The youth at once did his share to spread the alarm and, after returning home, joined his own company of minute boys, which was attached, in a sort of fashion, to Captain Parker's minutemen of Lexington. What the brave minute boys did during the battles of Lexington and Concord, the readers of the previous volume already know. Suffice it to say here that Roger and his chums, Dick Winthrop, Paul Darly, Andy Cresson, Ben Small, and a dozen others, fought as only those can fight whose souls are in their efforts. With all confidence, the British marched into Lexington and then Concord, only to be driven back along the road they had come, with the loss of many killed and many more wounded.

The various encounters of that never-to-be-forgotten day had left Roger with several wounds, none of which, however, were serious; and now, three weeks later, he was feeling nearly as well as ever, although he had taken the bandage from his head but a few days previous. Hen had suffered fully as much, and limped, rather than walked, as he resumed his duties.

Roger's adventures had not been confined entirely to the field of battle. During the day an attempt had been made to burn down Mr. Winthrop's house, and coming on the scene at just the right time, Roger had succeeded in rescuing pretty Nellie Winthrop from the flames. For this, Dick's sister was truly grateful, and said so, and her words caused Roger to blush deeply; for, although he had never breathed it to a soul, he thought Nellie just the dearest girl in the whole world.

The first hunt for the British detachment, after Roger's escape from the old stone house, had led the youth and his friends to the home of Uriah Bedwell, a pronounced Tory. As soon as it was ascertained that Bedwell was harboring the enemy, the man, who was known to be one of the meanest lawyers for miles around, was compelled to flee for his life, and his dwelling was burned to the ground, although with this destruction Roger had nothing to do. Uriah Bedwell fled to Boston, vowing vengeance upon all of his former neighbors, and especially upon Roger, whom he considered the prime cause of all his troubles. Of Uriah Bedwell we shall see and hear more later.

At the burning of the Winthrop homestead, a box containing some jewelry had been stolen by Barnaby Marston, a sanctimonious old hypocrite, who had been dubbed Deacon by those who knew him. Deacon Marston had tried to escape with the box, but failed, and he joined Bedwell in the flight to Boston. But he, too, was bitter against Roger, and hoping for a time when he might, according to his own notion, square accounts with the sturdy lad.

In a drawer of the old secretary that stood in the sitting room of the Morse house, Roger had placed a packet which he considered both sacred and valuable. It had been given to him by a British officer, Lieutenant Alan Brascoe, whom the lad had stumbled upon by the roadside, late in the day. The officer, lying at the point of death from a bullet wound in his breast, had begged that the youth see to it that this packet, along with his watch and money, be delivered to his wife, who lived in Boston. Roger had managed to retain the packet, but the timepiece and money had been confiscated by the British soldiers, who came up and made the lad a prisoner. Upon escaping and returning home, Roger had placed the packet, which was sealed up and addressed to Mrs. Constance Brascoe, in the safest place the house afforded. At present, with Boston in a state of siege, it did not look as if the boy would be able to keep the promise made to the fallen lieutenant; for he had determined, since the times were so uncertain, that, if the packet was to be delivered at all, he personally must undertake the mission. "I won't let the papers go out of my possession until I hand them over to Mrs. Brascoe," he told himself. "My word to the dead lieutenant must not be broken." Little did he dream of all of the adventures in store for him, for which that packet was to be largely responsible.

CHAPTER II

A PRECIOUS KEG OF POWDER

"ROGER!"

The call came from the gateway, directly after the noon hour, and looking up, Roger saw Paul Darly standing there, flintlock musket on his shoulder.

"I'll be with you in a minute, Paul," was the reply, and stepping back into the house, Roger brought down his own weapon from where it hung between two deer heads. "I'm off, Mother," he called out, and with a wave of his hand to his parent and Dorothy, he ran down to join his chum.

"Whar ye goin'?" came, in a shrill Yankee voice, and the tall form of Hen Peabody came into sight from the orchard. "Both armed, eh? 'Pears like ye wuz a-goin' to jine the minutemen down at Cambridge."

"Not just yet, Hen," answered Roger. "We are off on a hunt for powder."

"Gee shoo! An' whar do ye calkerlate to pick up

powder in these days, tell me thet? Why, powder is wuth its weight in silver now, an' before long it will be wuth its weight in gold, so Mr. Small was tellin' me."

"Roger thinks he has spotted a small keg of powder," answered Paul. "We are going to see if he is right."

"Perhaps I may be mistaken, but it won't do any harm to look," put in Roger, and told the hired man upon what he based his hopes.

"Wall, it's wuth investigatin', thet's sure," was Hen's slow comment. "But, boys, be careful whar ye go, for I have it from Jonas Anderson this mornin' thet the British have a number o' spies around here. If they caught ye with a keg o' powder they would kill ye— jest to git the powder away."

"We'll keep our eyes open."

"An' when are ye calkerlatin' to git back?"

"We'll be back by six o'clock, unless something unusual happens," concluded Roger, and then he and Paul made off down the road leading past the tavern and the meetinghouse and up a side path, which was a short cut to the old stone house they had in mind to visit.

"My, but what a day that was when we chased the redcoats back to Boston along this road!" observed Paul, as they hurried along. "Here is where Lord Percy came up with his reinforcements, and wasn't those other fellows glad to get behind his fresh troops and rest?"

"It was certainly a great day, Paul. But, to my mind, greater days are still to follow. Now we have driven the British soldiers into Boston, we haven't got them fast there, by any manner of means."

"Oh, I know that. But you musn't forget that our men are pouring in from everywhere, and before long we'll have a regular army stationed at Charlestown, Cambridge, Dorchester, and in between, and what are the British to do, then? They'll have to starve to death."

"Starve or fight; and it's my opinion they'll come out and fight, and when they do they won't make such a mess of it as they did at our town and Concord."

"Do you mean to say they can whip us, Roger Morse?" demanded Paul, indignantly.

"Whip us? You know me better than that, Paul. No, they can't—or rather they shan't—whip us. But another battle will be no child's play, that is what I am driving at."

"I do hope we find the powder. I heard Father say that powder was getting so scarce there was some talk of putting pikemen into the companies instead of fellows with flintlocks. It would be too bad if some of our gallant fighters had to give up their muskets and take to old-fashioned pikes."

"We'll get powder, somehow," returned Roger, confidently. "I heard somebody say they had sent to New York and other places for some. But those supplies may be a long time in getting here, since they can't come in by way of Boston Harbor. By the way, did Dick say anything about what is in the wind for next Saturday?"

"You mean the expedition to Hog and Noddle's Islands?"

"Yes."

"To be sure, and if you go I'm to go too. I was talking it over with my folks just before I came away. If we can't have powder those redcoats shan't have those hogs and cattle. Frank Nelson said he had heard fresh beef was up to four shillings a pound already. In another month I'll wager they can't get fresh beef in Boston at any price, unless some stores arrive from England, and I reckon by that time that we will have some vessels out to cut 'em off."

Allowing their conversation to run on in this fashion, the two boys presently entered the wood upon the opposite boundary of which the stone house was situated. It was a sunny May day, and the timber was alive with birds, while here and there sported a squirrel or a rabbit.

"How I would like to bring that fellow down!" cried Paul, as a rabbit popped up and gazed at them in wonder. "Doesn't he look as if he knew I didn't dare to waste my powder on him?"

"We can't afford to fire on anything excepting it be a redcoat—or a wolf," answered Roger, and he shuddered as he remembered the encounter he had had with a wolf at a spot not over a mile away.

The boys continued onward, until the edge of the wood was gained and the old house came into view. It was still deserted, and from the outside, looked just as it had on the day Roger had left it.

"Now we'll soon learn if I was right or not," said the youth, and shoved open the heavy oaken door, which creaked dismally on its rusty hinges. "Dark as pitch," he went on. "Paul, strike a light, will you?"

A flint and steel were quickly produced, and soon a bit of tinder was set ablaze, and then they lit a short candle that Roger had brought along.

"Windows covered with thick dirt don't let in much light," observed Roger. "However, I think this candle will do. Paul, hold it up as high as you can, and I'll climb up to that top shelf of the cupboard. What thick slabs of wood! The man who had this cupboard to build must have cut his boards with a broadaxe. If the keg is up here I'll soon have it out, and if it isn't, then we've come on a fool's errand."

"Oh, but I hope it—" began Paul, when Roger interrupted him with a low cry.

"Here is the keg, sure enough!"

"Hurrah!"

"Don't hurrah yet."

"But if you've got it—"

"It smells like dried fish."

"Oh, Roger!" Paul gave a deep groan. "Don't say we came away over here for a keg of decayed fish!"

"It looks that way—and smells that way, too, Paul. Look out, I'm coming down!" And as Paul stepped back Roger landed on the floor, hugging a fair-sized keg to his chest.

He had scarcely landed when a bung which was placed in one end of the keg popped out, followed by a small quantity of stuff which looked like fine black sand. Some of this struck the candle, and instantly there were half a dozen tiny flashes.

"It's powder!" yelled Paul, and as another flash went up he dropped the candle and fled to the doorway. "Come on, the thing is going up!"

The flashes around the candle also startled Roger, and his hold of the keg not being a very good one, the thing slipped from his grasp and rolled on the floor, close to where the candle lay spluttering. The powder began to pour from the bunghole, and light and explosive lay within a couple of feet of each other. With his heart in his throat, Roger followed after Paul, and both sped from the stone house for their lives.

"We—we—oh, how foolish!" burst from Roger's lips, when they had covered a hundred feet or more, and come to a halt on the safe side of a big elm tree. "To find the powder only to burn it up!"

"But why doesn't the keg explode?" questioned Paul, after a few seconds of silence. "I thought it was going up right away."

"So did I. I suppose the candle hasn't burned low enough yet. If only you hadn't dropped the light."

"And if only you hadn't dropped the keg."

"Well, don't let us blame each other, Paul. What is done can't be undone, unless—" Roger paused.

"Unless what?"

"There is still time in which to save the powder."

"What! Do you think to go back for it?"

Roger hesitated, expecting every minute to hear a tremendous explosion. "We might go back," he answered, as no shock occurred. "Maybe the light has gone out."

"I'd rather wait awhile longer."

"But then it may be too late, if the light is burning toward the powder. Come on—I'm going," and Roger started back for the house.

"Don't you do it, Roger; you'll be blown into a thousand pieces."

"It won't do any harm to take a peep."

"It will if the keg goes up just when you are peeping."

"I'll risk that. You needn't come if you don't want to."

Roger moved back toward the deserted house, and not to be thought a coward, Paul followed, but with legs that trembled so they could scarcely sustain him.

When the two came within sight of the dwelling, they paused again, and made a detour, which brought them in direct line with the half open doorway and the interior.

"Do—do you see—see it?" asked Paul, in a voice that trembled, in spite of all he could do to steady it.

"I can't see a thing," was the answer. "Both keg and light are behind the door, close to the cupboard."

"Can't you see anything of the light?"

"No; wait, I am going to try that window on the right," and Roger hurried off in the direction. He soon came to the opening. The glass was weather-stained, and full of cobwebs, but from the lower sash one of the little panes was missing.

Should he venture close enough to look inside? It would be taking a big risk, for if the keg of powder went up, the dilapidated stone house was certain to be totally wrecked.

"Don't you go; it's too risky!" shouted Paul, hoarsely. He had again retreated to the shelter of a tree.

But Roger was bent upon saving the powder, if the deed could be done, and waiting only an instant longer, he rushed swiftly up to the opening. One searching glance into the broad kitchen, and he hastened to rejoin Paul.

"Well?"

"The candle is still lit and lies flat," was the answer. "The keg of powder is two feet away from it, and about a handful of the powder is on the floor. It won't catch until the tallow runs over the boards and sets fire to it."

"Well, it won't take the burning grease long to do that. Let us get back," and Paul caught Roger by the arm.

"I'm not going to go back," was the reply.

"You're not? Why, Roger you can't be thinking of—" and Paul paused in horror.

"But I am thinking of saving the powder. Do you know what I'm going to do? Wet my jacket in yonder brook, creep into the house, and souse that light out, and I'm going to do it right now!"

CHAPTER III

"Roger, it's suicide!"

"I don't think it is—not if I hurry."

"But if the powder should go up—"

"It hasn't gone up yet, Paul." Roger threw off his powder horn and pulled off his jacket. "There is no time to waste." And with a bound he reached the tiny brook that flowed between the trees and wet the bottom of his jacket. "Now, I'm ready," and he started for the house again.

"Better come back," urged Paul, but the fearless youth paid no attention. He was going to save the powder if the deed could be done.

It must not be imagined that Roger was not aware of the danger he was running. He knew it only too well; and as he gained the doorstep leading into the broad and gloomy kitchen, the beads of perspiration stood out on his forehead, and he breathed a silent prayer to Heaven for deliverance from harm. It was only because he knew how valuable that keg of powder would be to the minute boys and men, that he ran such a fearful risk.

The kitchen floor was gained at last, and two yards away lay the candle and the powder, the former spluttering more furiously than ever, as the hot tallow ran in all directions.

Roger held the jacket in both hands, ready to shield his face should the explosion come—a poor protection, indeed, in case of such a disaster. Now he moved forward swiftly, but without daring to jar the somewhat shaky floor. The candle reached, he lowered the jacket over that fascinating blaze, and total darkness followed.

"Heaven be praised!" burst from his lips. Then he raised his voice joyfully. "Come in, Paul; it's out!"

"Are you certain?" came from outside.

"Yes, I'm certain. Strike another light, but be sure to keep it at a proper distance."

"Trust me for that. Roger, you're the bravest fellow I know of, indeed you are!"

"Don't spend time in praising me, Paul; strike the light, and I'll put the bung back in the keg, and see that it stays there. The powder on the floor we can put in our horns. This is a fine haul, for the keg holds all of twenty pounds."

"It will be a load to carry home. There is the light.

Better carry that keg into the open air before you bother with the powder in the floor."

"I will." Roger caught up the keg, hammered in the bung, and passed outside. "Won't the men be surprised when we distribute this among them?"

"Will you distribute it? It belongs to you, Roger."

"I don't think so, Paul. In the first place, I'm certain that Sergeant Kegan's crowd stole it from somebody living between here and Boston; and in the second place, I think that, in times like these, all the powder and ball we have ought to be divided up equally among the men and boys who are ready to fight for our side."

The keg deposited in a safe place, the two boys returned to the kitchen, and with the blade of a broad jackknife lifted up every grain of powder left, and transferred it to their horns. "If it is going to be worth its weight in gold, we can't afford to miss a smitch," remarked Paul.

"The sergeant never lived to tell about this powder," observed Roger, as they prepared to leave. "Poor fellow, he was a brute, but still it was awful the way he died, with a bullet through one eye."

"And two of his men were killed, too, weren't they?"

"Yes, a private named Patten, and another named Yorston. But Windotte, the fellow who put the keg up in the cupboard, got away with the rest of the troops to Boston." Roger mused for a moment. "He was an odd looking chap, that Windotte."

"How odd looking?"

"Why, he had such a queer, thin, pale face, and no hair on it. His skin was as soft as a woman's."

"Maybe he was a woman in man's clothing."

"Oh, no, I don't think that. I rather think he was just getting over a long spell of sickness. By the way, they say the smallpox in Boston is something awful."

"Yes, I heard that, too. If our soldiers catch the disease, it will go hard— Who was that?"

Paul Darly broke off short, as a form emerged into an opening ten paces away. As he pointed with his finger, the form disappeared.

"Did you see anybody?" demanded Roger, quickly.

"I did—a man. He is gone now."

"One of the minutemen?"

"I don't think— There is another, and another. Roger, they are coming this way, and they are strangers to me!"

Roger did not answer. But close at hand was a hollow, and into this he rolled the keg of powder, covering the article with some of the numerous leaves which lay scattered about.

The keg was scarcely out of sight when the three strangers strode up. They were good-looking men, well-dressed in shining waistcoats, ruffled fronts, and each wore a pair of cavalry boots with spurs attached.

"Hi, boys, what are you doing here?" demanded the leader of the three, as he stopped short in evident surprise.

"We are not doing very much," answered Roger, steadily. "And what brings you here, sirs?"

At this the three men frowned. "Zounds! Must we answer a boy's questions?" muttered one, in a low tone.

"We must be civil," answered his companion. "See, the young rascals are armed."

"Are you out hunting for redcoats?" said the leader, with a forced laugh.

"If we were, we wouldn't expect to find them here," replied Paul, promptly. "The redcoats, I imagine, know enough to keep inside of Boston."

"No doubt they do, lad. So you are out gunning, eh?"

"We haven't knocked over anything yet," returned Roger.

"I thought powder was too scarce for this kind of sport?" And now the leader of the three newcomers eyed Roger more sharply than ever.

"Powder is scarce, sir; still we have a little left— half a horn full," and Roger tapped the article mentioned. "We have to shoot with care, when we do shoot."

"Which way are you bound now?"

"We are working our way toward Lexington. Are you going on to Woburn?"

"What is that to you?" growled the man who had first demanded if they must answer a boy's questions.

His manner made Roger angry, and he straightened up stiffly.

"Haven't we as much right to ask questions as you, sir?" he said.

"Oh, that's right, lad, don't get angry," put in the leader of the newcomers. "Yes, we are bound for Woburn. You see, we were riding for that place when our horses took fright at the tavern and ran off. They belong in Woburn, and are certain to turn up there. Hope you have luck in your hunt after game. Good evening," and the man motioned for his companions to move off with him. The quarrelsome fellow still hung back.

"It's all nonsense, Becket," he said. "Cameron and I—"

"That's all right, Maxwell; come on," returned the man he called Becket, and after an instant's delay the three moved along, taking a course parallel to the brook, which ran between two small hills and then along the meadow adjoining the estate owned by Uriah Bedwell, the Tory who had fled to Boston after his mansion was burned down.

Roger and Paul remained standing where they were until the three men were out of sight. Each looked inquiringly at the other.

"What do you think of this?" demanded Paul.

"I think all is not as it should be," answered Roger. "Those men are strangers in these parts, and they wear city clothing. I'll wager a sack of grain they come from Boston."

"Perhaps we had better follow them."

"Just my idea, Paul. Wait a moment, until I hide this keg in the house again, so it won't get wet in case it rains, and I'll be with you. If those men are spies, our minutemen ought to know it."

The powder was soon returned to the old stone house, and then both boys hurried in the direction the three men had taken, being careful, however, to keep out of sight.

"If they see us and learn we are spying on them, they won't hesitate to do us foul," said Roger. "For as spies they'll know they carry their lives in their hands."

On went the party of three until the meadow before mentioned was gained. At a distance of a hundred and fifty yards stood the black ruins of what had once been Uriah Bedwell's costly mansion. Not so much as one stone or half burnt timber had been touched by the men who had driven him from the district. A short distance from the dwelling stood the spacious barn, also untouched, but empty of horses, cattle, and fodder, for the Tory had had some of his few friends transfer all to the besieged city.

"They are making for Bedwell's barn," announced Roger, from behind a convenient tree. "I believe the three are some of the Tory's city friends."

"But what are they up to?"

"That remains to be seen, Paul. Lay low now, for they may take a look around before they go in."

The two lads had scarcely dropped behind some brush before the three men paused and gazed about them. "They see us!" whispered Paul, excitedly, as one pointed in their direction. But he was mistaken; and a second later the men entered the barn, closing the big doors after them.

"Now what's to do?" demanded Paul, for he felt that Roger was the leader of the expedition, just as he was the leader in all that the minute boys undertook to do.

"I know what I am going to do," answered Roger. "I'm going up to the barn and find out what they are at."

"But if you get caught—"

"We have as much right to come here as they, haven't we?"

"But we said something about going toward Lexington."

"And they admitted being bound for Woburn. The Woburn road is a good half mile to the north of this place."

"They may say they lost their way."

"And we thought there might be good shooting in the meadow," laughed Roger. "Will you come along or stay here?"

"Oh, I'll go along," answered Paul, and without more ado the pair crept along the brush and the edge of the brook until the rear of the big barn was gained. Then they made a quick dash for the wagon house beside the structure.

They were now within fifteen or twenty feet of the three men, and Roger motioned for Paul to remain silent, at the same time tapping his musket significantly. There was a knothole handy, and to this the leader of the minute boys applied his eye.

He saw that one of the men had lit a candle and was holding it up, while the other two were at work on the slab flooring of the barn, one with a hatchet and the other with a flatiron crowbar. Drawing back, he allowed Paul to take a peep.

"Something valuable is under that floor," whispered Paul, a few seconds later.

Roger nodded, and took a second look. Soon one of the slabs of the flooring came up, revealing half a dozen ironbound boxes hidden underneath.

CHAPTER IV

THE DISAPPEARANCE OF THE ENEMY

"AH, men, here they are, just as Bedwell said we would find them," exclaimed the man called Becket, as the six ironbound boxes came into view. "Now if they contain what he said they did, we have made a rich haul indeed."

"Better open the boxes first," growled the man called Maxwell. "I wouldn't trust Bedwell under oath—the miserly lawyer that he is."

"Neither would I trust him," said Cameron, the third man. "But in this case he had an axe to grind. He was afraid to come for his plate himself."

"We'll soon know the truth. Help me lift the boxes up," returned Becket; and with the candle on an empty feed box, all three of the men started in, after another slab was removed, to hoist the ironbound boxes to the top of the floor. This accomplished, it was an easy matter to remove the covers, which had been secured in a hasty manner with only a few small nails.

By this time Paul had found a crack in the barn's side, and he was gazing on the scene as intently as Roger. Both boys fairly held their breath to catch every word that was being uttered.

"His plate," cried Cameron, as the first and second boxes were uncovered, revealing numerous articles of silverware, all of which had been thrown into the receptacles in extreme haste, as the packing, or rather want of packing, showed. "This stuff must be worth some money."

"Bedwell valued his plate at two hundred pounds," answered Becket. "Most of it came to him through his aunt, who was a Brascoe."

"A Brascoe?" queried Cameron, and Roger pricked up his ears. "Any relation to Lieutenant Alan Brascoe, who was shot down in the Lexington fight?"

"Yes, she was an aunt to him, too. That is how the Brascoes and Mrs. Bedwell fell heirs to that land down in New York. They say it's very valuable ground, too."

While talking, the men had uncovered the third and fourth boxes. Each was found to be tightly packed with pistols of the very latest English patterns. With the weapons were also several packages of flints.

"Now we are coming to the stuff that interests us!" cried Cameron. "If those traitorous minutemen had only known of this, how they would have rushed hither to arm themselves afresh!"

"It was a pity Bedwell could not get the loyal men of the neighborhood to arm themselves," replied Maxwell. "But I presumed the traitors watched them too closely. Now for those other boxes."

The covers came off as easily as expected, and there lay revealed, in one, two rows of twenty-four muskets, and in the other, five dozen powderhorns, each filled ready for use, with as many bullet bags to match, also filled.

"What a splendid company he could have armed!" cried Becket, as he surveyed the muskets, pistols, and ammunition.

"If only we can get all of this stuff safe into Boston," put in Cameron. "The more I think of it, the more I imagine we have cut out a big piece of work for ourselves."

"We will have to move with care," returned Becket. "But Briarley will have his team ready at eight o'clock tonight, and we can place the boxes under his household goods, and as he has a pass to move into Boston, the rest will be easy. What time is it now?"

"It lacks two hours of sundown yet."

"One of us ought to remain here, while the others can go on to Briarley's."

"Let us put the stuff back into place first—for fear some inquisitive minuteman comes nosing around." This was agreed to, and after lowering the boxes, the flooring was thrown into place. Then the men tossed up a sixpence piece among them, and decided that Becket should remain on guard, while Cameron and Maxwell journeyed on to the homestead of Josiah Briarley, half a mile distant. During the Lexington and Concord fights Briarley had remained a noncombatant. It was known that he was inclined to Toryism, but that he intended to remove himself and his household goods to Boston was news to Roger and Paul.

Taking care that they should not be discovered, the two lads watched the pair of men depart. Left to himself, Becket pulled from a pocket a flask of rum, took a deep potion, and then proceeded to make himself as comfortable as the bare state of the building permitted.

"We must get help, and without losing a minute," whispered Roger to his chum. "Come on," and he led the way to the brook and the brush.

"But where shall we go?" questioned Paul. "Almost all of the men are on guard duty around Boston, as you know."

"If it wasn't too far I'd go for Hen," answered Roger. Then his face brightened. "Mr. Winthrop and Dick are home. I'll get them. Paul, won't you go for Hen? You can run the distance in less than half an hour, I know you can. And the more men we gather the better; for we must not only overpower this Becket, but also capture Cameron and Maxwell."

"Yes, and Briarley, too, since he is in this plot to carry off these military stores," returned Paul. "Yes, I'll go for Hen," and in a second more he had started, running at the full speed of his sturdy, youthful legs.

The Winthrop homestead lay close to the side of a small hill, where the Concord road made a turn. As Roger had been there many times, and had approached it through these very woods, he chose the most direct path, and reached the place in less than twenty minutes.

"Why, Roger, what brings you here today?"

It was the voice of Nellie Winthrop, who called to him from the dooryard, where she was taking down some clothes that had been drying.

"Good evening, Nellie," he responded, and advanced toward her with a bright smile. "I came to get your father and Dick, if they are at home."

"And what is the matter? I saw you come out of the wood on the run."

"I have discovered three Englishmen, who are planning to remove some arms, ammunition, and plateware to Boston," returned the youth, quickly. "Are your father and Dick home?"

"We are," came a cry from the kitchen of the homestead, and Dick Winthrop showed himself. "Father, come here!" he called over his shoulder. "Roger Morse wants us."

Mr. Winthrop had been at work in the stable and

was just shedding a smock frock. He came forth with an anxious look on his face.

In as few words as possible, Roger related his story in detail, to which all, including Mrs. Winthrop, who followed her husband to the dooryard, listened with interest.

"To be sure, we must capture those men!" exclaimed the man, readily. "I will be with you in a moment. Dick, run down to the potato patch and call Nat Smith. He can go along. I'll get the two guns and the pistol. I think the best thing to do will be to capture that man at Bedwell's barn, and make him a close prisoner, and then lie low for the others when they come along with Briarley."

"But, husband, don't run too much of a risk," pleaded Mrs. Winthrop. "They may be desperate characters."

"We will take them by surprise," was the answer, and Mr. Winthrop turned away to get the weapons he had mentioned. His wife followed him, and this gave Roger and Nellie a few minutes to themselves.

"You are better," said the girl, half tenderly, as she looked at the wound on his forehead. I am very glad to hear it."

At this Roger blushed. "Yes, I am quite myself again, Nellie," he replied.

"Heaven be praised for it," said the girl, reverently. She was of old Puritan stock and deeply religious. "Dick tells me you think of joining Father in that expedition to Hog and Noddle's Islands," she went on, after a moment's pause. "Oh, Roger, do take care of yourself!"

"I will be careful, Nellie—since you ask it of me," he whispered; and then their hands met in a warm pressure which each understood thoroughly. "And you be sure to take care of yourself while I am away," he went on. Then Mr. Winthrop came out, and they separated.

Soon Dick came back on the run, with Nat Smith, a hired man, following. "Dick sez as how we're to fight some Britishers," said Nat Smith. "If so be I kin help, I goes along. I bees a true Liberty Boy, an' I wants 'em to know the same!" And he clutched the pistol his employer handed out. Smith was a Devon farmer, but since landing in Massachusetts four years before had been very bitter against his countrymen that had been left behind. "I came away to be let alone," he would say. "And so being as it is, what right have any of they to come over here to bother I?"

The party of four took the path Roger had pursued, moving along in Indian file, with the youth in advance. They did not run, but their walk was rapid. When the edge of the clearing was gained, and they came in sight of the barn, Mr. Winthrop halted his companions.

"See to it that your weapons are ready for use," he said. "Dick, you need a better flint than that," and he handed one over.

They were on the point of moving forward again, when they saw the man named Becket come forth and gaze around anxiously. Suddenly the fellow turned, and disappeared into the barn like a flash.

"He saw one or more of us," cried Dick. "What's to do now, Father?"

"Since we are four to one, we might as well advance upon the rascal," answered the parent. "He will see how foolish resistance would prove."

The four advanced through the meadow grass, their weapons held ready for use should there come a call to use them. Presently they stood at the barn doors, and Mr. Winthrop pushed them open.

"Come out of there, and give yourself up!" he called. "We are four to one, so resistance is out of the question."

To these words there was no reply, and now Roger pushed his way into the place with Dick following.

"He is gone!" cried Roger, after a swift look around.

"He can't be gone, for we saw him," answered Mr. Winthrop. "Nat, remain outside on guard, and you can go, too, Dick. He may try to run for it on the sly. Roger and I will hunt inside."

This plan was carried out; and while Mr. Winthrop remained below, Roger mounted to the loft. Fortunately, when going on a hunt for the keg of powder, he had carried two candles with him. He now lit the remaining one, and this gave him some light in a loft which, otherwise, would have been pitch dark.

"Do you see anything of him?" demanded Mr. Winthrop, after the youth had been hunting around for fully five minutes.

"I do not. Isn't he below?"

"Not that I can see. But he must be somewhere. Any loose hay for him to hide in?"

"Not a forkful."

"It is strange," mused Mr. Winthrop. "I wonder if he crawled out on the roof?"

He called to his son, and Dick and Nat Smith made a thorough tour of inspection. Nothing could be seen of Becket, and in a short while all of the party were convinced that he had left the vicinity.

"I'll tell you what he did," said Roger. "When he saw us coming from the wood, he ran back into the barn and out by that hole in the rear, and then off, keeping the barn between himself and us, so as not to be seen. The chances are that he is making for Briarley's house just as fast as he can leg it."

"But the guns and ammunition are safe, aren't they?" put in Dick, who felt sadly in need of a new musket and some powder. All of his powder had been consumed at the Lexington fight, and the stock of his gun had been shattered through being used as a club on a redcoat, who was trying to run off with a neighbor's silver service.

"Yes, all of the boxes are here," answered Roger. "Now if we— Hullo, here come Paul and Hen!"

"Whar air they?" came in a cry from the Morses' hired man, as he approached on a limping run.

"They ought tew be caught, an' Briarley, too, the mean skinflint!" burst out Hen. "I've had it in fer Briarley ever sence he swindled us on thet load o' musty corn," and the tall Vermonter shook his head decidedly.

The matter was talked over for a few minutes, and it was decided that Paul and Nat Smith should remain at the barn, guarding the boxes and keeping a watch for the possible return of the three Englishmen. Mr. Winthrop, Roger, Dick, and Hen were to lose no time in reaching Josiah Briarley's home, to head off the enemy at that point if it could be done.

CHAPTER V

The Confiscation of the Military Stores

"I Trust we catch this man Becket," observed Roger to Dick, as the two chums hurried along side by side. "Of course you remember that I am holding a packet in trust for a Mrs. Brascoe, the widow of that British lieutenant. Well, I heard this Becket mention the Brascoes. Probably he can give me just such information as I desire concerning the widow."

"Why don't you send the packet in through the guards at Boston Neck, Roger? They'll take it quick enough."

"No, I feel it my duty to deliver the packet personally. I would never forgive myself if I let it go and it got lost. I don't believe the siege of Boston will last very long. The British troops will grow tired of being penned in, and they'll come out and fight, or else we'll do some assaulting."

"Father thinks we have just seen the beginning of

this war, Roger. He says we'll have no easy time of it to wrench our freedom from England."

"I don't doubt but what he is right, Dick, for the colonies are too rich to let go without a fierce struggle to retain them. What a shame the mother country can't treat us fairly, and then we wouldn't want to break away!"

"King George and Parliament are acting very foolishly. I believe the majority of the English would gladly treat us better, were it in their power to do so. But now the first blow has been struck, it will be fight to the bitter end."

The journeys hither and thither since leaving his home that afternoon had somewhat tired Roger, and consequently, he could not push on as rapidly as Mr. Winthrop desired. "Leave me behind," he said, at last. "It will be foolish to wait for me and let that man Becket give his companions the alarm." And on the three went, Hen shouting back to the boy to take good care of himself.

"An' ef any o' them rascals appear, better shoot 'em on the spot," was the hired man's final injunction.

They were pursuing a footpath over a stony hill, and now, when left alone, Roger turned and made his way to the highway that ran past Josiah Briarley's residence. "No use of cutting a fellow's feet to pieces," he reasoned, for he wore nothing better than a worn pair of low buckle shoes.

The highway was gained, and he was wondering if the others had yet reached the rear of Briarley's home, when the sound of horses' hoofs came to his ears. He listened intently and made out three horses approaching.

"And from Briarley's house!" he murmured. "If it— The three Englishmen!"

The boy was right. The three Englishmen, booted and spurred, as previously mentioned, were riding toward him at top speed. As Roger had surmised, Becket had lost no time in reaching Briarley's house and informing his companions that their plan to remove the goods secreted by Uriah Bedwell was discovered. The one thought of the trio was now to get back to Boston in safety.

"I must stop them somehow," thought the youth, and his heart leaped into his throat. Then, seized with a sudden idea, he raised his musket and fired it into the air as a signal.

The unexpected shot caused the three horsemen to draw rein and gaze ahead inquiringly. They were still fifty yards from where Roger stood, and the youth had drawn to the shelter of some brush and trees. In feverish haste the old flintlock was reloaded, and then the boy waited for the next move on the part of those before him.

"Cameron, what does that mean?" demanded

Becket, somewhat nervously.

"I cannot imagine," was the reply. "Perhaps somebody is out gunning."

"Perhaps, but I don't like it. We are not such a great distance from Bedwell's house, remember."

"Don't stop here," came from Maxwell. "Every minute lost may prove our ruin. If those minutemen catch us they will not hesitate to string us up to the nearest trees."

"Oh, they are not quite so bloodthirsty as that," rejoined Becket. "Well, come on, but keep your eyes wide open and your pistols ready."

The three horsemen started ahead, but on a walk, with Becket gazing straight forward, and the others to the right and the left. Their pistols had been in their holsters, but now each kept his weapon in one hand while holding the reins in the other.

"Hold up there, please!"

It was a cry from Roger, and lowering his musket, he stepped squarely into view.

"One of the boys!" muttered Becket, savagely. "The one that brought the others to the barn." He raised his voice. "What do you want?" he demanded.

"I wish to speak to you," returned Roger. If only he could gain a little time he knew all would be well, for Hen would want to follow up the signal shot without delay.

"I haven't any time to talk to you," answered Becket. "Where are those others who were with you?"

"I don't know exactly," said Roger, telling the literal truth. "But I think there is some mistake here," he went on. "Were we to remove those stores for Uriah Bedwell, or were you hired to do it?"

"Why—er—what do you mean?" stammered Becket, while his companions gazed at Roger in amazement. "Did Bedwell say anything to you about the—the—you know."

"I'd like to know what he said to you first, sir. I think we must be working against one another without reason. You see, I and my neighbors know Briarley quite well. He's a good Teadrinker, too," and Roger gazed at Becket meaningly. In those days, when the patriots had refused to drink tea rather than use that which England had taxed, to say a man drank tea was equivalent to proclaiming him an upholder of King George III.

Roger spoke slowly, realizing that every second of time gained would be to his favor. He did not dare glance up the road behind the horsemen, but kept his gaze fixed upon Becket as the leader of the party.

"Boy, what is your name?" spoke up Maxwell.

"That doesn't matter, sir. I want to learn if we are playing a game of hide-and-seek between us."

"Perhaps we are—" began Becket, when a cry from

Cameron startled all three.

"Those others you spoke about are coming up!" yelled the horseman. "Don't believe what that youngster has to say. He is trying to catch us in a trap!"

Becket turned swiftly. Cameron was right. Hen, Mr. Winthrop, and Dick were coming up on a run, the Morses' hired man well in advance. As Hen came closer he raised his musket.

"Hold on thar!" he called out. "Hold on, or ye are all dead men!"

"To the infernal regions with them," muttered Becket, between his shut teeth. "Boy, you shall pay dearly for your ruse!" and raising his pistol, he pointed it at Roger, who had now leaped for the shelter of some trees lining the roadside.

The Englishman snapped the flintlock of his weapon and a loud report followed. But the aim was poor, the bullet merely clipping through the tree branch over Roger's head. Scarcely had the report died away than Hen fired, and Becket was seen to clap his hand to his left ear.

"I am shot! Forward!" he groaned, and started up his horse with a mad leap. Soon the three were galloping down the roadway in a bunch.

"Are ye hit, Roger?" came from Hen, as he proceeded to reload.

"I am not," was the answer, and then Roger discharged

his musket a second time, but now with the muzzle pointed at the trio disappearing in a cloud of dust. Mr. Winthrop and Dick also fired, and one of the horsemen was seen to throw up his arms and fall. A second later the horse of a second rider went down, pitching the man in the saddle over his head.

"One of 'em is goin' tew git away, ef he kin!" shouted Hen. "Somebuddy plug him!" But all of the muskets were empty; and before any could be reloaded, the rider dashed out of sight around a bend in the road. The man was Captain Henry Becket, he who had been shot through the ear. It was destined to be a long while before Roger should see this man again, and then under most trying circumstances.

Rushing forward, it was found that Cameron was seriously wounded in the side and had fainted. Maxwell had suffered a cut on the head when thrown from his steed, and sat on the grass much confused.

"Do you surrender?" demanded Mr. Winthrop, pointing his empty gun.

"I—I do," came with a groan. "Please don't shoot!" And Maxwell held up both hands in token of submission.

His pistol lay in the dust of the road, and Roger picked it up. While the youth relieved Maxwell of his other weapon, a long dagger, Mr. Winthrop, Hen, and Dick turned to aid Cameron. The wound was dressed and bound up as well as the means at hand permitted, and then three of the party, with Maxwell, carried the man to the nearest farmhouse. An hour later a doctor came to take charge of the case, and he had Cameron removed to the hospital at West Cambridge, where a number of the redcoats who had been wounded in the battles of Lexington and Concord still rested.

"And what do you intend to do with me?" asked Maxwell, anxiously; and when told he would be turned over to the proper authorities as a prisoner of war, he begged earnestly for his liberty, and even attempted to bribe Roger to set him free. But his proffers did not avail, and he was marched away, to be exchanged, three months later, for a minuteman whom the British held.

Before they separated, Roger tried to gain some information from Maxwell concerning the Brascoes, but failed utterly. "I don't know much, and what I do know I'll keep to myself," said the prisoner; and there the matter rested.

As soon as the wounded man and Maxwell were disposed of, several of the party returned to Uriah Bedwell's barn and removed the six iron-bound boxes from their hiding place under the floor. A strong wagon was procured, and the boxes were placed in this and taken to the Morse homestead. The muskets, guns, and ammunition were sadly needed by the minutemen, and the distribution which occurred the next day was one long to be remembered. The keg of powder was also brought from the old stone house, but by the advice of Hen, the contents were divided between the Darlys and the Morses. "You've given the public enough," said the long-headed Vermonter. "Keep this little— it may prove mighty useful before this difficulty comes to an end."

Josiah Briarley was astonished to learn that the plot to remove Uriah Bedwell's belongings to Boston had been so neatly frustrated. At first there were threats to make the semi-Tory suffer dearly for his part in the transaction, but as yet matters military and otherwise, were in a very unsettled state, and in the end Briarley moved into the city, taking with him his household goods, his family, and Bedwell's silver plate. But not so much as an old-fashioned pistol was allowed to pass the American guards at Boston Neck, nor a grain of powder or a single leaden bullet. All of such things were confiscated on sight, since the British were doing the same upon their side.

"And now for that expedition to Hog and Noddle's Islands," said Dick Winthrop, the day after the confiscated goods had been distributed. "I am awfully glad you are going along." He was addressing both Roger and Paul. "Mr. Small is going, and Ben, too, so there will be at least three or four minute boys along."

"And how many men will go?" questioned Roger.

"I don't know yet. That is to be decided when we get to Chelsea. You know the expedition is to start from there," returned Dick.

This was on Wednesday. On Thursday the party left Lexington, to meet the party from Chelsea on the day following, for the expedition to the islands had been planned for Saturday, May the twenty-seventh.

"Take good care of yourself, Roger," said Mrs. Morse, half tearfully, as she strained him to her breast on parting. "Remember, now your father is dead, you and Dorothy are all that are left to me."

"Don't fear for me, Mother," he answered. Then he kissed his parent and Dorothy, and shook hands with Hen, who wanted to go, but had been told to remain behind. The hired man's knee was very stiff from the run to Uriah Bedwell's barn with Paul. In another moment Roger had joined his companions on Lexington Green; and the expedition to Hog and Noddle's Islands was begun.

CHAPTER VI

HOW THE SIEGE OF BOSTON WAS BEGUN

WHILE Roger and his several friends are journeying from Lexington to Chelsea, let us look back for a brief period and see what had occurred in and around Boston since that memorable day, April 19, 1775, when, returning after an unsuccessful raid upon Lexington and Concord, the British troops, under Lord Percy and Colonel Smith, had been driven for miles along the country roads and over Charlestown Neck into Charlestown itself, where they finally rested under the protection of the British warships in the harbor; while the gallant minutemen took their stand, under General Heath, upon Charlestown Common, as the meadow at the upper end of the Neck was then called, and what is now known as Somerville.

When the British regulars left Boston in the morning, Charlestown was in a state of intense excitement, and this feeling grew as the news of the slaughter at Lexington and Concord came in. The schools were dismissed, stores closed, public buildings locked up, and many folks prepared to leave their homes. To add to the horror of the hour, it was learned that the Cambridge Bridge was down, so the redcoats would certainly come in by way of Charlestown Neck. Soon the firing was heard, and something little short of a panic followed, in which one schoolboy, Edward Barber, anxious to see what was taking place, was fatally shot.

"The British are killing off all the women and children!" was a cry which was taken up on every side, and now, unable to stand it any longer, many inhabitants took to the meadows leading to Medford and other places, while others ran for the clay pits behind Bunker and Breed's hills, there to go into hiding until morning. But the cry of a massacre was untrue, for the British molested no one saving those who took up arms against them. As soon as they could do so, they placed a strong guard at the Neck, and during the night nothing worth mentioning occurred. The next day the British, under General Pigot, returned to their quarters.

The tocsin of war had now fairly sounded, and from every town, village, and hamlet the patriots poured forth to fight the battle for liberty and independence. The Committee of Safety, as it was termed, issued a circular letter calling out the militia and urging the enlistment of men to form an army. "Our all is at stake," so ran the appeal. "Death and devastation are the certain consequences of delay." This circular was followed by a second, and minutemen and trained companies marched hotfoot to pen the British within Boston, or to do them mortal battle should they dare to come out again.

Because of their proximity, the Massachusetts troops were first on the scene, but others were quick to follow. Down in Connecticut old Israel Putnam was ploughing his field when news reached him of the outbreak at Lexington. Without an instant's delay he sped off on horseback to the principal towns of his state to spread the tidings and bring out all who were willing to shoulder a musket in the righteous cause. "Follow me to Cambridge as fast as you can," were his words, and he set off on a gallop for that town, and arrived there two days after the British retreat to Charlestown, having covered a hundred miles on one horse in eighteen hours!

And while the troops from Connecticut were thus getting together, word had been sent up into New Hampshire, and soon the militia came pouring down to Haverhill Ferry, and from thence made their way by the Andover route to Cambridge. Little Rhode Island was also heard from, and her troops came in under the generalship of that well-known fighter, Nathaniel Greene. From two thousand the army gradually rose to sixteen thousand men.

Yet this body was an army only in name, from a

military standpoint. Nine men out of every ten were simple farmers or backwoodsmen, knowing little or nothing of military matters outside of some slight "trainin'" secured on the local village green. Uniforms were almost unknown, and what was far worse, less than fifty percent were properly armed. How scarce powder and shot were we have already learned.

But these patriots had two things in their favor. Those who could shoot at all could shoot well, and every one of them was used to untold hardships and to facing perils such as were new to the well-housed and well-fed soldiers of King George III, sent over to subdue them. They were willing to fight until the last ditch and until the last charge of powder was used; nay, they proved, later on, that they could fight even after the last ditch was passed and the powder horn had long since been drained. "They did not understand when they were whipped," so one English writer expressed it—for the simple reason that they never considered the battle at an end so long as victory was not upon their side.

At first all was confusion among the forming army, but gradually, through the efforts of Doctor Warren and Generals Ward, Heath, Putnam, and others, the militia and minutemen were formed into regular companies and regiments, and sent to guard Boston Neck, Cambridge, Charlestown Neck, Chelsea, and numerous places between these points, which lay in a grand semicircle around Boston. For several weeks the guards at some points were decidedly light, but gradually they grew more secure, until Boston was cut off entirely from the rest of the world excepting by water.

The state of affairs brought about by this siege was a curious one. Here were the patriots, besieging thousands of their friends, as well as their enemies. As Boston was thus cut off, provisions became scarce, and soon the town was threatened with a famine. Inside of the place it looked every day as if there might be a serious riot between the citizens and the British soldiery. What to do became a serious question.

The British commander, General Gage, knew he could not feed so many long, without the public larder giving out, and he also knew that a starving man will fight, no matter what the consequences. So it was decided that all who wished to do so could leave their arms and ammunition behind, and move out of the town by way of Boston Neck, the inhabitants of Charlestown being also allowed to depart, under similar conditions, by way of Charlestown Neck. At first these fleeing people were allowed to take their household effects, but, as conditions grew more and more desperate, this was denied the patriots. In return for this favor, those who lived on the outside, and were of royal tendencies, as Josiah Briarley, were allowed to take their worldly goods, also minus arms and ammunition, and enter Boston.

As the American army, or perhaps more properly, the New England army, settled down to the work before it, fortifications were thrown up at various points, first in the vicinity of Cambridge, and then at the other points being guarded. While this was being done, the food question was eagerly discussed, and to obtain rations for our army, as well as to cut off the British, it was decided to bring within the American lines all of the hogs, sheep, and cattle, as well as the hay, to be found on the various islands in the harbor.

The people in Boston were also considering this subject, but a large fire on the seventeenth of May put the plan out of their heads for the time being. However, on the twenty-first of that month, an armed schooner and two sloops left the town for Grape Island, the intention being to bring away the stray cattle, and a large quantity of hay, the latter to be used for the British cavalry horses.

The expedition moved to the island with all possible caution, but in the midst of their labors, the British troops were discovered at the cocks of hay by several men of Weymouth, who raised the alarm by ringing the bells and firing muskets. Soon all the men of that village, and of Hingham and Braintree, gathered on the shore, and as speedily as the flood tide permitted, a sloop and a lighter were floated, and filled with minutemen, who set sail for the island. On the sloop was one of the sons of Mr. Adams, then at the head of the provisional government of Massachusetts, and he was the first man ashore. A fight at long range followed, and the British fled as fast as they could for their ships, and returned to Boston. The minutemen burnt up all the hay in sight, also a large barn, and brought as many of the cattle as could be rounded up to Weymouth.

The affair on Grape Island had occurred on Sunday. Two days later Mr. Winthrop got word of it, and also that the Americans intended on the following Saturday to go to Hog and Noddle's Islands, to bring off whatever might be found there. On one of the islands were pastured twelve head of cattle which the farmer had purchased at a round price only the fall previous. "I don't want to lose them," he told his wife, and immediately arranged to join the expedition, satisfied that he could easily prove his own property after the raid was finished. Of course Dick could not be left behind, and how Roger and the other minute boys joined in has already been related.

CHAPTER VII

THE EXPEDITON TO HOG AND NODDLE'S ISLANDS

"Do you look for any opposition at the islands?" questioned Roger of Mr. Winthrop, as the entire party journeyed forward on its way to Chelsea.

"Certainly there will be opposition if the British discover what we are up to," was the answer. "We will, however, move to the islands and back as quickly as possible."

At this period, Hog and Noddle's Islands, since much filled in and otherwise altered, and now known as East Boston, were little more than immense pastures and orchards, separated from the mainland at Chelsea by a muddy channel which, at low tide, was less than three feet deep. A ferry ran to the islands, and shallow boats made frequent visits for the benefit of the few people living on Noddle's Island Hill and the vicinity.

After crossing the Medford, or Mystic River, the party moved directly for Chelsea, stopping on Friday night at the farmhouse of a friend, named Grossbeak. This man was an underofficer among the minutemen of Chelsea, although, as a plain farmer, he disdained the title of lieutenant, which had been conferred upon him. He was to lead one of the detachments to the islands, and having cattle of his own there, mixed up with the heads belonging to Mr. Winthrop and a dozen others, he was, of course, more than ordinarily interested.

"We'll go over between ten and eleven o'clock in the morning," he said. "I have a flatboat, and so has Caleb Dickson, and we have a sloop and any number of small boats, besides. I don't reckon there will be enough to bring away everything of value, and give the redcoats a good shaking-up in the bargain, if they show themselves."

"I don't want any fighting," said Mr. Winthrop, "but I'm going to have my cattle, cost what it may."

"Parsons tells me that one of the British men-of-war has moved up pretty close to Noddle's Island," went on Grossbeak. "We'll have to keep an eye on that ship."

At nine o'clock, after a hearty breakfast of corn cakes and bacon, served by Mrs. Grossbeak and her four daughters, the party set off for the Chelsea flats. It was a clear, warm day. All wore their boots, for they knew they would have to wade through considerable mud and water. Each man and boy of the party, which numbered ten, under Grossbeak, was, of course, armed, and carried from six to sixteen rounds of ammunition. Six rounds of powder and ball may not seem many to some of my young readers, who are accustomed to going into the woods and blazing away, regardless of the waste; but they must remember that, in the days gone by, these things were not so plentiful, and a hunter had to make the best of what he possessed. Grossbeak himself carried but six rounds, but as he had on more than one occasion gone into the woods with but four rounds, and brought down two deer, and once a bear and a deer, it could well be said that this crack shot had all that was necessary.

The flatboat which the lieutenant possessed was amply large to hold the ten who entered it, and once on board, two of the men seized their poles and quickly sent the craft over the water in the direction of Noddle's Island, the pasture farthest from the mainland. It was felt by all that, once the cattle and other livestock were driven from Noddle's Island to Hog Island, the rest would be easy, as the enemy would scarcely dare to venture close to the Chelsea shore.

The sloop previously mentioned held on board sixteen men and boys, and this party was the first to land on the farthest island, although Grossbeak's crowd was not far behind. Once on land, all set off to round up all the cattle and sheep in sight. It was a work with which everybody was familiar, and it progressed rapidly. Naturally Roger, Dick, and Paul kept together, and soon they became separated from their older companions, as the work of driving in the livestock went on.

"There is one of our cows," cried Dick, presently, as he pointed to a peculiarly marked beast. "Isn't she a beauty? I know Mother and Nellie will think a sight of her, when we drive her in. Nellie loves a good-looking cow."

"I like a good-looking cow myself," returned Roger, feeling he must somehow second the choice of the girl who filled so large a portion of his thoughts. "There are four more, Dick, on the other side of the ditch."

"And there is one behind the patch of brush," added Paul. "Hi, hi! Cush, cush!" he called out, as the cows grew alarmed, and started for the southwest end of the island.

"Let us round them up from the left, that will be the easiest way," said Roger, and they set off as rapidly as the treacherous state of the pastureland permitted.

The work was well in hand, when suddenly there came a shot from the hill near the center of the island.

"What does that mean?" exclaimed Paul.

"It's a signal," answered Dick. "The redcoats must have discovered us!"

"Let us run down to the shore and make sure," burst out Roger.

They had just started to run when the low boom of a swivel gun came from over the waters of the harbor. "That's from a man-of-war!" said Dick. "No use of going farther. The quicker we get back to Hog Island the better!"

"Boys, boys! Take care of yourselves, the redcoats have discovered us!" came from a distance.

"What about the cattle?" called back Dick.

"We must let them go, or kill them."

"Kill our cows! Not much; I'm going to save them if I can!" returned Dick, stoutly.

"And I'll help you," said Roger. "The enemy must be some distance off as yet, and if we go around the hill we'll be out of the range of that cannon on the ship."

As rapidly as it could be accomplished, six of the cows belonging to Mr. Winthrop were rounded up. The others could not be found. "I think they must be on the upper end of the island," said Dick. "They once belonged to John Race, and his cattle are up there. Come on!" And away he went, with Roger on one side, and Paul on the other, driving the beasts before them at the top of the animals' speed.

"Aren't you fellows coming back?" came the cry, a few minutes later, and Ben Small, who had gone off with his father, appeared.

"To be sure we are coming, Ben, but we are going

to bring these cows," answered Roger. "Have you seen anything of the enemy?"

"Father has his marine glass, and he saw them. They are coming over in a schooner and a sloop."

"How many of them?"

"Father counted two boatloads, about forty or fifty. He thinks they are marines from one of the warships," continued Ben.

"If that is so we'll have a hot time of it presently," said Dick, with a shake of his head.

"Never mind, Dick. We fought at Lexington and Concord, and we can fight again," said Roger.

"Hurrah, that's the talk!" came from Paul Darly. "Down with the redcoats, say I!"

Several shots rang out, some from the water, and an equal number from the minutemen on the island. The alarm was now general, and as the British marines drew closer and closer it soon became apparent that to drive off all the sheep and cattle to Hog Island would be impossible, while to take away the salt hay was entirely out of the question.

"If we can't have them, the redcoats shan't have them, either!" was the cry, and shortly after torches were set to the cocks of hay, and a barn that was full, and they were burnt to the ground. An old farmhouse was likewise burnt, and a good many cows and some horses were butchered, the carcasses of the cows being thrown into the flames that the British might not carry them off for provender.

All this, of course, took time, and meanwhile the boys drove the six Winthrop cows well toward Hog Island. Here they met Mr. Winthrop and Mr. Small, and learned that four of the other cows were likewise safe. "The other two, I reckon, I can give up as lost," said Dick's parent.

As rapidly as possible the British schooner and the sloop landed their marines, forty in number, and these naval soldiers came on, firing as they ran. Soon some of the other men-of-war lying in the harbor sent out men, and about noon there was quite a detachment of the British on Noddle's Island and around it.

"They are going to chase us into Chelsea!" was the cry of the minutemen.

"We'll see if they do!" came from Grossbeak; and as quickly as it could be done he organized the cattle drivers into several detachments, one of which was posted close to the west shore, another by the road, and the third in a ditch near the point for which one of the enemy's small boats was heading.

The boys were with the detachment in the ditch, and waited with thumping hearts for the coming of the enemy.

A shot signaled their approach, coming from the boat, and singing through the air directly over Ben

Small's head. "Gosh! But that was close!" muttered the minute boy, and without stopping to think twice he fired in return, and saw one of the rowers let fall his oar.

A full volley from the small craft answered Ben's shot, but nobody in the ditch was hit. The boat was still some distance away, Ben having reached his mark only by chance. Soon, however, the craft came so close that each individual on board could be plainly distinguished.

"Now for it!" cried Roger, in a low voice, and all in the ditch, saving Ben, who had not yet reloaded, fired together. Two of the marines went down, and one of them slipped overboard, but his comrades hauled him back. Whether any of the shots had proved fatal those in hiding could not tell.

It had not been expected that the ditch was to be held permanently, and as the marines advanced, the minutemen and the boys fell back from one point or another, always keeping out of sight as much as possible behind meadow grass, bushes, and trees. Yet the force of the enemy was constantly growing, and presently a rush was made, in which the worthy Grossbeak received an ugly wound in the head that put him in bed for four months afterward. Mr. Winthrop was also hit in the leg, but the wound was of small consequence, and did not stop him from taking part in the remainder of the battle.

So far the boys had kept pretty well together, but now, as they sped on toward the narrowest part of the channel between the two islands, Roger and Dick sped in one direction, and Paul and Ben in another.

"I must say I am getting hot!" exclaimed Dick as he came to a halt under the shade of a maple tree. "I didn't expect quite such a run as this."

"Nor I," returned Roger, bending down to get a drink from a spring near the tree. "Bah! That water is half salt," he exclaimed, a second later. "Now I'll be more thirsty than ever."

"There is a good spring up on the hill, Roger. But I don't know as we dare venture that far. Yet I don't see any marines just now."

"They have halted near the ditch, Dick. I can see two heads over the brush. After such a warm reception they'll be cautious as to how they advance."

The two lads decided to mount the little hill to the spring, and go down on the other side. They moved from tree to tree, and bush to bush, having no desire to expose themselves for targets, even at such a distance as now divided them from the redcoats.

The spring gained, another disappointment awaited Roger. The stones around the place had been thrown down, and a dead sheep lay in the bubbling water. "They might have let this be," grumbled the lad. "But I suppose

Grossbeak didn't want to leave any accommodations for those Britishers. Come," and on they went again.

The eastern slope of Noddle's Island was in sight, and they were congratulating themselves that no enemy had sprung up to bar their progress, when Roger, on looking behind, saw Ben Small running toward them as rapidly as his short legs would carry him.

"Roger! Dick! Stop!" screamed the young fellow. "Stop, I say!" and as he came closer the others saw that he had a deep scratch on his left cheek, from which the blood was flowing freely.

"What is it, Ben?" questioned Roger, quickly. "Did the redcoats do that?

"Yes—no—I can't say. They collared me, and I broke away after kicking one of 'em in the ribs!" came from Ben, pantingly. "But poor Paul is a prisoner still!"

"A prisoner!" burst from Roger and Dick, simultaneously.

"Yes, a prisoner, and two marines have been detailed to march him off to one of the small boats."

"Gracious, this is too bad, Ben!" said Roger.

"Can't we rescue him?" put in Dick. "Only two marines, did you say, Ben?"

"Yes, two, but they are big and strong fellows, I can tell you that. I can't understand yet how I got away. They have my musket and my powder horn."

"Are the two men alone? I mean, have the rest of

the party left them entirely?" went on Roger.

"Yes, they're alone. But—"

"Then let us go after them, Dick. We can't leave Paul this fate without making some effort to save him."

"It's awfully risky, Roger—"

"Then if you don't want to go—"

"I didn't say that. Yes, I'll go, but we must be cautious." Dick turned to Ben. "Do you care to go back and show us the way?"

"I would if I had a gun or something."

"Here is a pistol Father loaned me. But you must be careful of it, Ben, for it's a fine French weapon, as you can see. Better wash your face in yonder pool, and there is a spider's web you can put over the scratch to stop the flow of blood."

"We don't want to lose time," said Roger, while Ben was washing, with Dick getting the spiderweb, which hung over some brush. "Those marines may put off in the boat, and then the jig will be up."

"No; the orders were to hold us at the boats until the other marines came back," returned Ben. "I'll be ready in a minute more," and he was, the thick web stopping the flow of blood almost instantly.

And then, to save their friend, the boys began as daring an undertaking as they had experienced since the memorable encounter at the Morse milkhouse on the day of the battle of Lexington.

CHAPTER VIII

The Encounter at the Spring

The boat to which the two British marines had taken Paul Darly lay in a little cove on the west shore of Noddle's Island, not far from where there was a small clump of elm trees.

The boy's hands had been bound behind him and his musket taken from him. On the way to the boat one of the marines, to make him move the faster, had kicked him in the right leg, and this hurt considerably.

"It wasn't fair to kick me so," said Paul, as he dropped on one of the seats of the boat. "As a prisoner of war I—"

"Hold your tongue!" interrupted the largest and heaviest of the marines. "We don't take back talk from a rebel, especially from a boy."

"What are you going to do with me?"

"Take you to the ship, and then hand you over to General Gage's officers in Boston."

At this announcement Paul gave a shiver. He had heard how badly American prisoners in Boston were faring, and had no desire to join the number of unfortunates.

The youth sat in the middle of the boat, with one marine behind him and the other in front. The fellows were in a thoroughly bad humor, for they knew they would be severely reprimanded for having allowed Ben to escape.

"It was your fault, Munson, that the other lad got away," said the big marine, at length.

"And I say it was yours, Biggs," was the angry response. "You had hold of him."

"Yes, but why didn't you run after him as I told you?"

"I had hold of this lad."

"You should have run. It's a fine story we will have to tell to Captain Clancy—that two men couldn't hold two boys."

So the talk ran on for fully ten minutes, until it looked to Paul as if the two marines would get into a pitched battle, as each was already shaking his fist in the other's face. But finally Biggs cooled down, and to appease his larger comrade offered him a drink from a pint flask which he carried. The treat made the two as much of friends as ever.

"Let it go," said Biggs. "I'll tell the captain a clever

tale that will smooth it all over. We had to fight four rebels, remember," and he winked suggestively.

"Yes, we had to fight four rebels, and all well-armed," said Munson, and nodded that he understood perfectly.

"And what if I tell the truth?" questioned Paul, with more boldness than prudence. At once Biggs gave him a heavy slap on the ear.

"You'll keep your tongue between your teeth, lad," he growled. "If you don't—" He ended with a fierce look and a shake of his brawny fist; and then Paul said no more.

The drink of fiery liquor had made Biggs thirsty, and as there was no more in the flask he began to cast around for a drink of water. "Munson, did you notice if there was a spring anywhere around?" he asked.

"There is a spring up behind yonder trees," was the answer. "If you go up, fill the flask," and he handed over the article in question.

Leaving Munson on sole guard at the boat, Biggs sauntered slowly off, his big gun slung over his shoulder, and the flask in his right hand. For some time not a sound had come to him of any fighting, and he surmised that friends and enemies were half a mile or more away.

"I trust the boys whip the rebels thoroughly," he mused, as he moved along. "If they do Captain Clancy will be in fine humor, and he'll let the escape of that boy go by unnoticed. But if they don't come back successful, why then I fancy I'll have warm work ahead to keep out of the brig for neglect of duty."

The trees gained, he began a diligent search for the spring. He had moved along for a hundred feet when he fancied he heard a strange noise from his left. "Who's there?" he demanded, coming to a halt and catching hold of his musket.

No answer to his question was vouchsafed, and after waiting for fully a minute in breathless attention, he concluded that he had been mistaken. "Pshaw! I must be getting nervous!" he muttered. "I wish I had a mug of flip to steady me! But, heigh-ho, flip is not to be had, nor brandy, nor even hard cider, so for once water must do—if the confounded spring can be uncovered."

The big marine advanced ten yards farther, and now came to the spring, from which flowed a tiny stream of the coldest and purest water to be imagined. Throwing his musket down, so that it might not slip forward and get wet, he bent down for a drink. It was certainly more refreshing than the liquor had been, and he took a deep draught. He had just finished, when a shadow in the rear startled him.

"What is th—" he began, turning about to find himself confronted by three boys, including the one that had broken away from him.

"Silence, if you value your life!" came from Roger,

who had been watching the boat for several minutes, and had mapped out a plan of action for his chums.

"But what does this—this mean?" stammered Biggs, falling back as Roger's musket was pointed full at his face. His own gun was gone, and he now noticed that Ben had it.

"Silence, I say," repeated Roger. "If you make the least outcry your life will not be worth a shilling."

"So this is your lay," said the marine, bitterly, turning to Ben. "I wish the captain had shot you instead of making you a prisoner!"

"Perhaps we had better shoot you instead of making you a prisoner," replied Ben grimly, and he, too, pointed his musket, or rather the marine's weapon, at Bigg's head. Dick's weapon was likewise raised, and the three muzzles certainly made a determined showing.

"For the sake of Heaven, don't shoot! Please don't shoot!" burst from the marine. "I—I surrender, if that is what you want. Put the guns down; they might go off accidentally."

"If you surrender drop that powder flask, and clasp your hands together behind you," commanded Roger.

"Yes, but—"

"Do not ask questions but do as I ordered," went on the boy coldly, and without lowering the barrel of his musket an inch.

With a rattle the flask struck the stones about the

spring, and Biggs placed his hands as he had been commanded. His face was twitching nervously, and it was easy to see that he felt himself to be in a bad situation. Once a wild thought entered his head to make a dash for liberty, as Ben had done, but he was not brave enough to take the risk.

"Now, Ben, bind his hands behind him with the rope I gave you," said Roger. "Mind you bind them so he cannot slip them apart."

The rope in question was one the boys had brought along for possible use on a refractory cow. Soon Ben announced his job complete, after which Biggs was marched away from the spring to where the trees were thick. Here he was made to back up against a sturdy walnut, and was bound fast.

"Now listen," went on Roger. "We are going to leave you for awhile. If you keep silent all shall go well with you, but if you dare to cry out, we'll come back and finish you."

"Are you going to rescue that other lad?"

"Do not ask any questions; but remember what I told you," returned the leader of the minute boys; and then he and his two chums moved off.

"He'll keep mum enough," said Dick, when they were out of hearing. "For a fellow that must weigh two hundred pounds, he's the biggest calf I ever met."

"Here is your pistol, Dick," said Ben. "I have his

musket, and it's a first class affair, by its appearance. Now what's to do, Roger?"

"Don't show yourselves until I have looked over the ground," was the answer.

The edge of the wood was gained, and all looked across the stretch of meadow to where the boat lay in the cove. They could readily see Paul with his hands tied behind him, and Munson, who was looking in the direction of the spring.

"We might as well make a dash," began Dick, when Roger pulled him back.

"Wait just a moment," whispered the latter. "See, the marine has turned, and is gazing out over the water." He leaped up and waved his musket. "If only I can signal to Paul that we are watching for a chance to get to him!"

He continued to wave his weapon, and Dick and Sam did the same with their muskets. Suddenly Paul caught sight of them and leaped up. "He sees us!" cried Dick. "Oh, gracious, look at that! Paul has tipped the marine into the water! Come on, boys, now is our chance!" And he set off on a run.

The report was true; Paul had caught sight of his chums, and as quick as a flash understood the meaning of their unexpected appearance. The chance to get clear of Munson had been too good to be lost, and one sharp shove, accompanied by a lurch of the rowboat,

"COME ON, BOYS; NOW IS OUR CHANCE!"

had done the trick. Munson went down in less than three feet of the briny element, and came up minus his head covering, and with his eyes and nose plastered with black mud.

"You villain!" he spluttered. "I'll—I'll kill you for that! Whow! What a mess!" and he started in to clean out his eyes as he waded ashore.

As the marine went overboard, Paul leaped for land, and reaching it, set off on a dead run for his friends, who as quickly headed in his direction.

"Paul, are you all right?" were Roger's first words, when they came together.

"I am. Unloosen my hands," was the answer, and the minute boy was quickly liberated. "Oh, how glad I am that you came!"

"We must get away as fast as possible," put in Dick. "All of our men are moving back to Hog Island. If we are not sharp we'll be cut off from them."

"Yes, we must lose no time," said Roger. "Paul, do you think you can run?" he added, as he noticed how the boy was limping.

"I can't run very fast—I got an awful kick," was the answer. "You go ahead and I'll follow."

"No, we must keep together. Down, all of you, down!"

All fell to the ground, just as a musket shot rang out. Munson had secured his weapon and fired it, but the leaden messenger passed over their heads.

"I'll give you one for that," cried Roger, and fired in return. The marine was struck in the arm, and his weapon fell from his grasp.

The echo of Roger's musket had scarcely died away, when there came to their ears a call from the hill upon which the spring was located. The call was answered from several points in the wood, and a party of a dozen redcoats appeared. It took them but a moment to sight the boys, and then they bore down upon our young friends.

"We are trapped!" groaned Ben, who was the first to see the enemy.

"Trapped?" queried Dick.

"Yes, trapped. Look ahead."

Roger and the others looked, and their faces fell.

"We can never get through that line alive," murmured Paul. "We are in for it now for certain!"

"Don't give up yet," said Roger, who was reloading with all possible speed. "Perhaps we can escape by running along the shore, if we hurry." He looked at Paul. "Paul, can't you run at all?"

"Not very far. But go ahead, don't mind me," was the truly brave response.

"We won't leave you," came from all of the others in a breath.

"Let us stand and fight, if we must," added Dick.

"That won't do—with only four against a dozen or

more," interrupted Roger. "I have another idea, boys. Let us take to the boat and row around to Hog Island. Of course we'll run the risk of a shot from yonder man-of-war, but that's better than facing the British on this island."

"But that marine?" began Dick.

"We'll take care of him in short order," was the confident reply. "Come ahead!"

And turning, the little party of minute boys ran for the cove, Roger, Dick, and Ben in advance, and Paul bringing up in the rear as rapidly as his sore limb permitted.

CHAPTER IX

The Man behind the Driftwood

When Roger spoke about taking care of Munson he remembered that the fellow had fallen overboard, and that, in all likelihood, the marine's ammunition had become wet. This was the truth.

As they raced toward the boat, Roger and Dick pointed their muskets at the marine's head. "Off with you!" yelled Dick, and fired. The bullet merely cut the air. Then Munson aimed his weapon at Dick, but the hammer hit the flint without a report following, and he threw the musket away in a rage. A second later he was running for the woods, where he now beheld his own party on the return to the boat.

"Why don't you fire at him?" cried Dick, impatiently.

"He is running; let him go," was Roger's calm return. "I may be sore pressed for this round of ammunition before this day is over. Hark!"

They listened and heard Biggs yelling for someone

to come and release him. "I only hope they stop to do it," said Paul, after being told of how the big marine had been made a prisoner. "See, two of the fellows are turning back."

"We mustn't lose a second," went on Roger, as the cove was gained. "Into the boat with you!" And as the others followed his directions, he ran back and caught up Paul. Soon all four were on board of the craft, which was then shoved away from the soft meadow bank.

There were oars aplenty, a pair for each minute boy, had they desired so many. But all of the lads were more used to plough handles than oars, so they only took one apiece. "We've got to make Hog Island somehow," said Roger.

"Down with the oars, and each make a stroke as I count," and he began in measured tone. "One, two, three, four," and off they went, rather zig-zaggy at first, but doing better with every stroke.

It must not be supposed that the British marines had stood looking on without doing anything to stop them. Down they came to the cove on a run, several firing as they advanced. But the aims were poor and no harm was done; and by the time the water's edge was reached, the rowboat was two hundred yards off.

"Come back, ye rebels, come back!" roared Captain Clancy, who was in command of the detachment. "Come back, or my word for it, all of you shall be hung!"

"We're not coming back—not just now, anyway!" answered Paul, and leaping up, he fired Ben's musket at the British officer. The shot tore through Captain Clancy's three-cornered hat, and somewhat alarmed, the British officer fell back several paces, at the same time ordering a second volley aimed at the courageous lads who had thus taken their lives in their hands in order to escape.

The round was quickly forthcoming, but the minute boys were on the watch, and the rowboat being plenty large enough for the purpose, they dropped behind the gunwale just as the order to fire rang out. Spit, spat! Several bullets struck the boat, but only one passed through, doing no damage.

"Anybody hurt?" questioned Roger, and receiving a satisfactory response, made an inspection of the hole. It was just above the water's edge, so no plugging was needed, and once again they started to pull as energetically as before.

"We are doing well," said Roger, fifteen minutes later, when the cove had been left behind, and they had turned the western spur of Noddle's Island. "That detachment is worse off than we, for they haven't any boat in which to return to their ship."

"Don't crow, for we are not yet out of the woods," answered Paul. "See, that man-of-war over yonder is beginning to move this way!"

"She can't stand in very far," put in Ben. "The water shoals rapidly over here. But they may give us a shot."

They continued to pull, until Hog Island could be seen, not over a quarter of a mile ahead. Then from the man-of-war came the booming of a cannon, and the water in front of the rowboat spurted up like a geyser.

"They're training their guns on us, lads!" exclaimed Paul. "That was rather a close shave."

"A miss is as good as a mile, Paul," rejoined Roger, as cheerily as he could. "But pull on, before they blow us to pieces."

"Oh, I hope we don't get another shot!" cried Ben, and it must be confessed that his voice trembled just a bit. And he can hardly be blamed, for the situation was truly alarming.

The beach of Hog Island was still fifty yards off when another gun roared out. Then came a crash as the ball struck the stern sheets of the rowboat, and on the instant all of the boys found themselves floundering in the water. "I can't swim—I'll drown!" spluttered Paul, and then he stood up rather sheepishly, for the water proved to be less than three feet deep. Gathering up their muskets and other effects, they went splashing through the water and mud to the shore, Roger helping

Paul along, and Dick carrying the weapons of the pair. The rowboat, with its stern completely shattered, was allowed to drift off at the mercy of the tide.

"Thank God, we are out of that!" said Roger, when they had gained the shelter of some trees, and the other boys said amen. It was not likely that they would ever forget that voyage. "If that last shot had come two feet nearer—" shuddered Dick, and it was not necessary to finish, for all understood him only too well.

"Where in the world have you boys been?" The cry came from their rear, and turning, they found themselves confronted by Mr. Winthrop and Mr. Small.

"We just escaped from Noddle's Island in a boat," said Dick. And in a few words he gave the particulars. "I'm afraid I didn't save those cows, after all," he added, soberly.

"Seven of the cows are safe; the others we'll likely never see again," said the father. "But you have had a narrow escape. Come, the British are following to this island as fast as they can, so we must lose no time here."

Mr. Winthrop led the way, and the entire party followed, through an orchard and across a long stretch of meadow. Here were fully half a hundred farmers and minutemen driving a large number of cows, horses, and sheep before them. All told, the livestock numbered about six hundred heads; certainly a bunch worth the saving, as Mr. Small declared.

The first body of marines from the British war vessel had now been increased by detachments from several other ships, and it looked as if a battle worse than that at Concord was at hand. All Chelsea was aroused, and the minutemen began gathering at Chelsea Neck, where the livestock were being driven over to the mainland. As the warships could not come very near on account of the shallow water, they sent out barges mounting swivel guns, and these began to send in their shots at a lively rate.

"We are in for it, men!" cried one of the captains in command of the Americans. "But hold your places, and we will soon have reinforcements."

"Here comes Doctor Warren!" was the sudden cry, and a moment later Doctor, afterward General Warren, came dashing up on his charger. The doctor was the best known and best beloved of all the patriots in and around Boston, and his coming created great enthusiasm.

"Keep them back, boys!" he shouted, "Keep them back! General Putnam will soon be here with some of the militia. Keep them back!"

"We will, doctor!" was the reply, and a hurrah rang out as the impulsive physician seized a musket, and let fly at one of the barges, which was coming in close to Hog Island. A dozen reports followed, and the gunner on the barge, who was on the point of discharging his heavily loaded swivel, fell back, wounded in two places. So hot was the fire of the minutemen and boys, that at last the barge had to turn about, and stand off a hundred and fifty yards farther from the shore.

The sun had gone down and it was growing dark, but still the firing continued at odd intervals. Men and boys were tremendously hungry and thirsty, but food and drink was forthcoming in abundance, the women of Chelsea appearing with baskets and trays piled high with good things. "Eat all you will!" was the cry. "But don't, under any circumstances, let the British land here!"

As it became darker, the minutemen and boys were spread out alongshore as a picket guard. It was a clear night, so all could see some distance across the still waters of the harbor.

"I wonder how long we will have to remain here," observed Roger to Dick, as the two paced the marsh at the water's edge.

"I'm sure I don't know, Roger. I suppose those reinforcements will arrive sooner or later."

"I'm glad we've got the livestock off. Four or five hundred head of cows and sheep would keep Boston in meat for some time."

"I understand they are going to go to the other islands soon," went on Dick. "But this will serve as a warning to the redcoats, and I reckon they will be for capturing what is left as quickly as possible."

Here the conversation lagged, and each boy resumed his picket route. Roger had just made his turn, when a dark object, floating about a hundred feet from the shore, attracted his attention.

"I wonder what that can be," he asked himself, and, coming to a halt, he surveyed the object intently. "It looks as if it might be that wrecked rowboat. "More than likely it is."

However, to make certain, he continued to watch the floating thing. That it was composed of some boards there was no doubt, but it did not look altogether like a rowboat, even a half smashed one. At last he called Dick.

"It's a bit of driftwood," said Dick. "But it's odd it doesn't come to shore like the rest of the stuff floating about."

They continued to watch the object, and presently, to their surprise, saw it move away from them even more rapidly than it approached.

"I'll wager there is a man behind that woodwork!" cried Roger, struck with a sudden idea. "He is trying to get ashore unobserved!"

"If that's the case, let us challenge him."

"I hardly think it will do any good, since we have no boat in which to go after him. I have another plan.

Come with me." Roger raised his voice. "I'm going back to town. I'm tired of playing the fool out here."

Dick understood the ruse instantly. "So am I going back," he said, in an equally loud voice. "Let somebody else play guard here if he wants to."

Side by side they hurried away from the marsh to a road leading to Chelsea. The road was lined with trees, and behind the first of these they sought shelter.

"Now, unless I am greatly mistaken, we'll soon see something worth watching," said Roger.

With strained eyes the two boys crouched behind the trees and waited. They were now so far off that the object in the water could scarcely be discerned.

"It's coming this way!" whispered Roger, a few minutes later. "It's driftwood, but there is somebody behind it, just as I thought!"

He clutched his musket tightly, and Dick did the same. Slowly the object came nearer to shore, until at last it struck in the mud close to the reed grass. Then from the rear the form of a man came into view, a tall individual, wearing the clothing of a private citizen.

Reaching the dry ground, the man proceeded to shake the water from his clothing. This done, he struck off toward a side road leading to Salem.

Without uttering a word, Roger motioned for Dick to follow him, and both sped across an adjoining field. This brought them out on the side road at a point several rods in advance of the stranger, who was coming on at a rapid gait, his coat buttoned tightly about his neck, and his hat pulled well down over his forehead.

"Halt!" commanded Roger, as the man drew near. "Halt, or I fire!"

"Oh, dear me!" came in half a whine. "Don't— don't—shoot, I beg of you!"

"Why, it's Deacon Marston!" exclaimed Dick. "What in the world has brought you here in this fashion?"

CHAPTER X

If ever there was a surprised individual, that individual was Barnaby Marston, the old hypocrite who had escaped to Boston, after trying to steal the Winthrops' rosewood jewelry box.

"Dick Winthrop," he faltered. "And Roger Morse! Where—where did you come from?" And his teeth began to chatter with combined cold and fright.

"We were watching you from the shore, Marston," replied Roger, who had been as much amazed as his chum. "Do you surrender or not?"

"I—surrender? What—what do you m-me-mean?"

"I mean what I say. I consider you an enemy of our colonies, and I call upon you to surrender, as a prisoner of war."

"But, boys, this is a—an imposition," came from the so-styled deacon. "I am no enemy, as you must know."

"You are an enemy," answered Dick, readily. "You must surrender, or—"

"Or what?"

"We will fire at you." And Dick again raised his musket, which he had allowed to drop, upon making his unexpected discovery.

A howl of sheer fright went up from Barnaby Marston, for the sight of a firearm completely unnerved him at any time. "Don't! Don't!" he whined. "I—I'll give in— anything—only take away that gun!"

"Have you a pistol with you?" asked Roger.

"No."

"Dick, you had better search him and see. I will continue to keep him covered."

At this, Marston's face fell more than ever. "Morse, don't be so hard upon me, I beseech you. I—I am not the bad man you take me to be, I can assure you."

"Perhaps you'll say you didn't steal that jewelry box," returned Roger, coldly.

"I—I—that was a mistake, as I tried to explain to you down in your orchard."

"There was no mistake about it. You intended to take it to Boston if you could. You are no better than a common thief."

"You are cruel to say that, Morse, indeed, indeed you are," returned the hypocrite. "To tell the truth, the battles at Lexington and Concord so bewildered

me that I did not know what I was about. I was—"
Deacon Marston broke off short, as Dick tried to get
into an inner pocket. "Must you really search me like
this? I have nothing of value on me—only a few things
of my own."

"Dick shall search you from head to foot. Go ahead,
Dick, and if he resists, I'll make it warm for him," and
Roger tapped his musket significantly.

The demonstration with the musket nearly caused
Barnaby Marston to collapse, and the search went on
without more trouble. But as it progressed it was plain
to see the man grew more and more nervous.

"He hasn't any pistol," announced Dick. "Here is
a watch and some shillings and pence, and a five pound
note, and some keys."

"Is that all?"

"Here is a notebook and some letters, one of them
sealed up. I can't make out the addresses."

"Put them all into your pocket, Dick; they may prove
of value."

"Are you going to rob me?"

"No, but I think it best to turn over your notebook
and the letters to the officers here."

"And what will you do with me?"

"We shall turn you over also; eh, Dick?"

"To be sure."

"But I have done no wrong."

"That remains to be proven. What were you doing in the water?"

"I—er—I fell in."

"Fell in? Where?"

"At Noddle's Island. I was visiting Mr. Williams there, when the battle started, and I hurried to get away. I missed the road and fell into the water, and catching hold of some driftwood, came over to the mainland."

"That's a likely story," returned Roger. "If you fell overboard at Noddle's Island, what you would do would be to scramble back to land as fast as possible. My private opinion is that you came ashore from one of the British ships, and for no good purpose. I shall hand you over to— Hullo, what's that?"

A loud shouting on the road had interrupted Roger. The shouting continued, and now all heard the tramping of foot soldiers and of horses.

"The British are coming!" came from the shore, and at once all became excitement. This report was not true, but its effect upon Roger and Dick was disastrous to their plan concerning Deacon Marston.

"If it's the British, we must get out of here," exclaimed Dick, and turned to look up the road. Roger did the same, and taking advantage of the momentary excitement, Barnaby Marston leaped into the brush which lined the roadway, and disappeared from view.

"He's gone!"

"Where did he go to?"

"Over to the left."

"Shall we follow him?"

"Wait a minute. If the party approaching are British, we had better clear out in double-quick order!"

The two boys waited, holding their muskets ready for use. Nearer and nearer came the foot soldiers and the horsemen.

"Hurrah! It's General Putnam with the reinforcements!"

"And they've got two cannon with 'em! Hurrah!"

The news was true. General Israel Putnam, that stirring old "warhorse" of Connecticut, had come on the scene with two field pieces and three hundred men. As soon as they were certain of this, Roger and Dick set off on a hunt for Marston, but the rascal had taken time by the forelock and made good his escape.

"Never mind, we have his letters and his notebook; they may prove valuable," said Roger.

But now was no time to examine the things, for alongshore all was bustle and excitement. The British schooner, filled with marines, had come up close, and was firing random shots along the Chelsea waterfront. As soon as possible, General Putnam had his two field pieces trained upon the vessel.

"I call upon you to surrender, or I will sink you!" called the general, and the cry of surrender was taken up on all sides.

"We didn't come in to surrender. Take that with our compliments!" was the answering cry, and there followed two round shot, one of which tore up the ground directly between Putnam's field pieces, covering his gunners with dirt. Without waiting any longer, the American cannon were discharged, and a constant firing was kept up for the greater part of two hours. While this was going on, those in command of the schooner lost control of the craft, and she stuck in the mud. At eleven o'clock the firing from the British ceased.

"They are abandoning her!" was the welcome announcement, and it proved true. Finding themselves unable to get the schooner off, and being unwilling to remain in such an exposed position during daylight, the British left the craft just before midnight, and in several small boats, betook themselves to the larger war vessels in the harbor.

This ended the battle, if such it may be called, for Saturday and the night following. Early on Sunday morning a party of a dozen men, headed by one Isaac Baldwin, went on board of the schooner, stripped her of her guns, ammunition, sails, and stores, and then burnt her. This was done under a constant fire from the British sloop previously mentioned, and also from an attack from Noddle's Island, and this brought on a second engagement, lasting until Sunday noon, when

the British withdrew, with a total loss of about ten
killed and wounded. On the American side none were
killed and only five wounded. The contests enriched
the colonists to the extent of twelve swivel guns, four
4-pound cannon, and a highly acceptable quantity of
powder and shot. It may be added here that, soon
after, another expedition was organized to Noddle's
Island, and also expeditions to Pettick's Island and to
Deer Island, which were also successful. But in these
expeditions our minute boys took no part.

It was well on toward daylight Sunday morning when
Roger and his chums were released from duty. They
were thoroughly tired out, and Mr. Winthrop had directed
Dick to take the cattle to the pasture of a friend in
Chelsea. The friend's name was Carington, and Mr.
Winthrop was certain that at this farmer's home all
could find resting places for the balance of the night
and as long as they might care to sleep.

"I must deliver these letters and the notebook first,"
said Roger. And he hurried off with Dick to the captain
in command of the minutemen of Chelsea, not knowing
where General Putnam was, and concluding that this
officer would not care to waste time over Barnaby
Marston's affairs.

A brief examination proved that the notebook
contained but little of value. In it were a number of
private accounts, showing, only too well, what a miserly

man the so-called deacon was. "He'd beat a widow out of her mite if he could," said Dick, as he glanced over the pages of the book.

The letter that was sealed seemed to be of some importance, for the Chelsea captain read it carefully several times. "Perhaps you young men can tell me something of this," he said. "The water has caused the ink to run, and it makes hard reading."

The letter was signed "U. B.," and was addressed to "My dear Windotte." Only about half of it could be made out, running as follows:

"Marston will carry this to you. I told him he would find you at Buckman's tave . . . and if not, he will look for you at some house in the neigh . . . was a good plan to use a woman's dress, but if . . . information will be valuable, and we . . . eral Gage expects to learn . . . hundred pounds, or more . . . by Monday night. . . . urs faithfu . . .—"U.B."

"Kind of a riddle, eh?" said the captain, as Roger studied the letter.

"It is and it isn't!" burst out Roger. "I think I can see through the millstone."

"What do you make out of it?"

"The writer of this letter is Uriah Bedwell, the Tory, whose house was burnt down over near Lexington."

"I see. Well?"

"The man called Windotte is a British soldier. He helped to capture me once, and I remember him well. He had a smooth shaven face, and looked for all the world like a woman."

"And you think he is masquerading as a woman?"

"I do, and he is either at Buckman's tavern in Lexington, or at some farmhouse near it. Marston was to go to him, deliver this letter, and then get some information, for which General Gage expected to pay pretty well."

"I believe you've struck it, Morse."

"To be sure he has struck it!" put in Dick. "The British have tried this same game before. Only last week they caught a man in woman's clothing, up at Marblehead. He was spying around, trying to find out how much of an army we had in that district."

"If this is true, we should do something to catch this Windotte," said the captain of the Chelsea minutemen.

"Yes, and right away," said Roger. "Remember, Barnaby Marston is at liberty, and probably he will try to give this Windotte the alarm. I reckon the best thing we can do is to get back to Lexington without stopping to sleep here."

The matter was talked over for several minutes, and Mr. Small, Mr. Winthrop, and half a dozen others were called in. As it was not known what the British intended to do in and around Chelsea, it was thought best not to allow too many of those who had come in from Lexington to depart.

"I will take care of the cattle and remain here," said Winthrop. "Dick and Roger can go and tell the men at home, and they can take care of this case;" and so it was settled, and a few minutes later the two chums set off, as tired as before, it is true, but still eager to do anything which might further the cause of the colonies' independence.

CHAPTER XI

THE VISITOR AT THE MORSE HOMESTEAD

"I WONDER how Roger is getting along."

It was Mrs. Morse who spoke, as she lay down her well-worn Bible, which she had been devoutly reading during the time that Dorothy had been absent at the Sunday morning service held in the Lexington meetinghouse.

"I hope he is all right, Mother," was the girl's reply, as she cast off her shawl and bonnet and prepared to set the table for their dinner. "Somebody at church said there had been a fight at the islands, but nobody was sure of it."

"There was cannonading during the night, I am certain of that, but it may have come from Charlestown."

"We will soon know, for Roger expected to be back by tomorrow night, unless something detained him," rejoined the daughter, as she passed from the sitting room into the kitchen.

The dinner was already on the table, and Mrs. Morse was saying grace, when there came a loud rap from the front door knocker. For a second the mother paused, then finished her prayer. "Go, see who it is, Dorothy," she said. "Perhaps some neighbor has brought news."

The daughter hastened to the wide oaken door and threw it open, to find herself confronted by a tall female, plainly dressed and wearing a deep bonnet of black.

"This is Mrs. Morse's home?" asked the newcomer, in a low tone.

"Yes, madam," answered Dorothy. "Will you be pleased to walk in?"

"Thank you," was the return, and the tall female entered the wide hallway. "I trust I am not asking too much at your hands, but I was told by Mrs. Channing, of Salem, that I might stop here, and if I mentioned her name I could rest assured of a welcome. I would have stopped at the tavern, but I am traveling alone, and there are so many rough men about—" The lady did not finish, but Dorothy understood her.

"Mrs. Channing sent you here?" questioned the girl, in a puzzled way.

"Not exactly that, Miss—Morse—am I right?" Dorothy bowed. "Miss Morse, not exactly that. But you see, it is this way. I am traveling to Dorchester, to join my brother, who has just entered the army. I had to come on alone, and I made one stop at Mrs. Channing's, and she said that if I did not care to wait at Buckman's tavern for my brother to come for me, I might apply to you. Of course, I am willing to pay for the accommodation, and if you will only take me in, I'll be a thousand times obliged to you in the bargain."

"Well, I—I will bring my mother to see you," answered Dorothy, hesitatingly. She had looked the newcomer squarely in the eyes, and the gaze returned far from suited her, it was so cold and crafty. "Pray, take a seat," and she motioned the applicant to a high backed chair standing near the long hall clock.

It was not necessary to summon Mrs. Morse, who already stood at the entrance to the dining room, and who now came forward. At once the newcomer offered a thin, white hand. "I am Norah Devore," she said, introducing herself. "My brother is a lieutenant in one of our Massachusetts regiments, with his company stationed near Dorchester Heights." And she repeated what she had already told Dorothy. "If I can only stay here until my brother comes for me I will pay you well," she concluded.

"And when do you expect your brother?" questioned Mrs. Morse, and at the same time looked at Dorothy, in an endeavor to learn what her daughter thought of the proposal.

"He said he would come Monday night or Tuesday, if possible. He may, however, keep me waiting longer, for, as you know, in these times, it is hard for any army officer to get away."

"I presume that is so." Mrs. Morse hesitated. "What do you think, Dorothy? You see, since I became a semi-invalid, my daughter runs the house, and as the work would fall entirely upon her—"

"But I will pay well—" insisted the newcomer, for a third time.

"It is not a question of money," put in Dorothy, with her eyes still on that unusual face. "We are not in the habit of entertaining folks here, least of all strangers."

"Then you refuse to take me in?" was the tart return. "It is decidedly uncharitable, to say the least. In these days, the tavern is no fit place for a lady traveling alone."

"We might give Miss Devore a room and her meals until Tuesday," said Mrs. Morse, as she turned aside with her daughter, her tender heart touched. "I would not wish to go to the tavern, were I traveling alone."

"I don't like her looks—they are not honest," murmured the girl.

"But Mrs. Channing sent her here," returned the mother, in an equally low tone.

"We have only her word for it. She may be a thief, or worse."

"We must not be uncharitable, child. We can watch her closely while she remains."

"As you will, Mother, but I hardly approve of it," and Dorothy gave the newcomer another close scrutiny.

A few minutes later the newcomer had laid off her shawl and bonnet and was seated at the dinner table. She had professed to be very hungry, but now ate sparingly of the humble Sunday fare provided, for in those days a sumptuous Sabbath meal would have been looked upon as something of a sacrilege.

The newcomer had brought a large handbag, and this was taken to a pleasant room on the second floor of the house. Miss Devore had asked particularly for a front room, "So that I can watch for my brother," as she put it, and this was given her. She said she would lie down to rest, having journeyed a long distance the night before.

"She is very agreeable, Dorothy," was Mrs. Morse's comment, when the two were in the kitchen alone.

"She is, so far as her speech goes, but there is something about her general appearance that I do not admire," returned the girl.

Hen had been out to the pasture, looking after a cow that had sunk into a bog hole. "Got a border, have ye?" he grinned, after Mrs. Morse had told him. "Will, I reckon ef she wants tew keep quiet she hed better keep away from Dorchester. There air goin' to be mighty lively times in Dorchester, Cambridge, an' Charlestown afor long, fer sartin."

Immediately after his dinner was despatched, Hen walked up to Lexington Green, to learn if there was any news from the front, for in those exciting times the news was carried everywhere as quickly as possible on horseback. The hired man was particularly anxious to hear from Roger, who was the apple of his eye.

"Ef anything happens tew thet boy I'll never forgive myself fer lettin' him go off without me," he mused. "Gosh, but I must be a-gittin' tew the front soon or my old flintlock will be growin' rusty. I wish Doctor Warren or Mr. Adams would order a raid on Boston—we'd soon wipe out them pesky redcoats," and he began to hum an old-fashioned colonial song to himself, running somewhat in this fashion:

> "King George's men are coming on,
>   To make us pay the tax O!
> We'll never pay a penny in,
>   The bullies we will wax O!
> We'll run 'em out of Boston town,
>   An' hang 'em by the heels O!
> We'll tax their coffins and their plot
>   An' ask 'em how it feels O!"

Around the green and the tavern quite a number of boys and elderly men were gathered, the middle-aged being largely at the front. A rider from Charlestown had just come in, and while he was getting refreshments he told of what had happened during Saturday afternoon on Hog and Noddle's Islands. "They were still at it when I left, and I'm afraid the redcoats are getting the best of it."

This news put a damper on the enthusiasm, but many did not believe it. Soon the rider was off, on his way to Concord, and after chatting with some friends for half an hour, Hen prepared to return home. As he was about to leave a faraway roll of a drum greeted his ears.

"A New Hampshire regiment is coming!" was the cry, and men, women, and children came running from every direction. It was an unusual sight to see a whole regiment from another colony, and especially on a Sabbath day. Soon the regiment appeared, coming down the road on a route step, with drums beating, fifes whistling, and banners flying. The officers were on horseback, and all presented a soldierly appearance, even if the men were but half-uniformed and half-armed.

"We're going to the front to teach old Gage a lesson!" was the cry. "Don't hang back! Come along!"

"I'll be with ye soon!" shouted Hen, as he waved his hand at one company after another. "If ye git the chance, see ye wax 'em good!"

As the regiment passed the Morse homestead, Hen followed the last company, keeping step with some of the men to ask where they were from, and what particular district they were going to guard. But the men could not tell where they were going.

"I left hum in a mighty hurry," said one. "Wuz cuttin' down a walnut tree an' got her half through. She's got to stand thet way till I git back." The man's name was Silas Codman, and it may be mentioned here that Codman went all through the Revolutionary War, and came home, after four years' absence, to finish cutting down the very walnut tree in question.

As he approached the homestead, Hen noticed Dorothy and her mother at the front door, waving their hands. Then his gaze traveled to the window of the upper room the stranger was occupying. The sight that met his gaze filled him with interest. The lady sat close to the opening and was apparently counting the soldiers. In her lap lay a tablet, upon which every few minutes she put down some figures.

"She's most mightily interested," was Hen's mental comment. Then, as the soldiers drew out of sight down the road to Charlestown Neck, he sauntered over to a field opposite the house, that he might get a better view of the upper room. "Ef Miss Dorothy don't like her it won't do no harm to spy on her a bit," reasoned the Vermonter, whose bump of inquisitiveness was as large as his nasal organ was long.

In the field was a large elm tree, and standing behind this it was easy for Hen to see without being seen. He saw the lady writing rapidly in a small notebook, which she soon after slipped into her bosom. Then she arose, and, placing her handbag on the bed, began to unlock it.

"Goin' tew shake out her dresses, I reckon," he murmured, when he saw something which astonished him greatly, for from the bag, which was a commodious one, the lady drew a pair of man's knee breeches, a waistcoat with ruffles, a pair of long silken hose, and a pair of buckle shoes to match.

"By gum!"

For the moment Hen could say no more, for his breath had been almost taken away. He continued to watch, and saw Norah Devore replace the articles in the handbag. The lady retreated to the rear of the apartment, and though he was not certain, he imagined that she removed the long mass of black hair with which her head had been covered.

"Now what in creation is she a-doin' with them air man's clothin'?" thought Hen. "An' ef thet hair ain't her own why is she a-wearin' of it, like an actor on the stage? I must allow ez how I don't like this fer a shillin'. Reckon I'll tell Miss Dorothy wot I seed," and without delay he started for the back door of the homestead, making a wide detour for that purpose. He managed to find Dorothy alone, Mrs. Morse having lain down to rest, for the doctor had told her that the more she kept quiet the sooner would she become entirely well.

"Yes, it is very odd, Hen," said the girl, when the hired man's tale was finished. "But it may be possible the clothing is for her brother. I do not like her at all, but—but—what are we to do?"

"Don't do anything—only let me put in a leetle time keepin' an' eye on her," returned the hired man; and so it was arranged.

CHAPTER XII

HEN PEABODY INVESTIGATES

LATE in the afternoon the stranger announced that she was going out for a walk, and asked Dorothy to accompany her, knowing full well that the girl must remain at home to wait on her mother, who had just experienced one of those strange sinking spells which came and went without warning. "If I am not back to supper do not wait for me, since I am not hungry," said the odd looking lady, and walked off.

Hen was around the kitchen at the time, whittling out some jackstraws with a sharp knife. Whistling softly to himself, the lean Vermonter put away his whittlings and his blade, put on his hat, and sauntered off likewise, but by a back path. He saw the lady take to the road leading to Bedford, and by running along the stone walls and trees to the left of this highway easily kept her in sight without being seen.

Nearly a mile was passed and the lady reached a

small cottage occupied by a very old man named Darrel Kirk. Kirk was known to be "a hard customer," having been both a drinker and a fighter in his day; but now he was over eighty years of age, and he had declined to take sides in the present controversy between the colonies and the mother country. "I fit enow in me time," he would say. "Onless they be laggards let the younger blood settle the matter—I'll have nay o' it," and he was left alone, to do as he chose.

Coming up to the door of Darrel Kirk's home, the lady knocked loudly three times, and then three times more. There was a bustle within, and presently a small wicket near the top of the door was opened cautiously.

"Who bees knockin'?" came in Kirk's shrill tones. He was a good deal of a hermit, and hated to be disturbed.

The lady replied in a low tone, so that Hen, even though he had come quite close, could not hear what was said. There followed a conversation lasting several minutes, after which the door was opened and the lady entered the house.

"This is most mysterious, tew say the least," mused Hen. "This ain't no oncommon call, not by a jugful. I reckon I hed best see wot she an' old Kirk air up to."

With great caution Hen walked around the house, which was set in the midst of a grove of maple trees. To his chagrin, every door below was tightly shut. The windows were also closed, and over them Kirk had either drawn shades or hung up bits of old flour sacking.

"He ain't goin' fer to be spied upon," went on the Vermonter, meditatingly. Then he looked at the upper windows. One of them was partly open, and it was close to an outstanding branch of a sturdy tree.

The proximity of the window to the tree branch gave Hen an idea, and in a trice he was mounting the tree. Crawling out on the branch, he caught hold of the windowsill and from this dropped into the bedroom beyond.

Having proceeded thus far, the Vermonter paused, considering what his next move might be. From below came the low murmur of voices. Straining his ears, he caught a few words, but being disconnected, they were unintelligible to him. However, he made certain that three people were talking, and he wondered who the third party might be.

The bedroom was piled high with odds and ends of furniture, boxes, and barrels, the accumulation of years, for Kirk was one of those persons that believe in saving everything, even if it is a hat without a crown or a pair of boots without soles. Picking his way among this rubbish, Hen descended the enclosed staircase leading into the kitchen below. The door was ajar, and by the voices the Vermonter learned that the talking was being done in the front room. Pausing only an instant, Hen slipped into the kitchen and behind the door leading to a narrow pantry.

"It is very hard to get the information, Captain Rembrandt," the lady Hen was watching was saying. "That last regiment was exactly four hundred and sixty men strong, and of those less than three hundred were armed."

"And what of that regiment you met at Salem?"

"That contained nearly five hundred men, and over four hundred were well-armed."

"And where were the regiments going?"

"The one from Salem was bound for Cambridge. I haven't found out anything about the other regiment yet."

"And about those army orders you were to beg, borrow, or steal from Captain Wilkney?"

"He is a thorough rebel, and I could do nothing with him. But give me time and I'll get the information, as sure as my name is Henry Windotte," returned the party dressed as a lady.

"By gum!" muttered Hen. "I half suspected it, but git me ef this ain't carryin' the spy business putty fur. Won't I jest land on Mister Henry Windotte fer imposin' on Mrs. Morse an' Dorothy! He shan't git back tew Boston tew tell about it nuther," and the Vermonter shut his teeth hard.

"I am instructed to get all of my information in as soon as possible," said Captain Rembrandt, who will be remembered by readers of the former volume as having been at one time a confederate of Uriah Bedwell.

"And what of that plot to capture Doctor Warren and Samuel Adams?" put in Darrel Kirk, in his treble voice. "To my mind, thet's an oncommon fine trick to be played."

"All in good part, Kirk, but keep your mouth closed, or you'll get into trouble with your neighbors."

"Trouble? Oh, no, nobuddy will hurt old Darrel," squeaked the old man. "I'm too old to take part in this trouble, indeed I be!"

"But ye ain't too old to allow these redcoats an' spies tew use yer house fer a meetin' place," muttered Hen, wrathfully. "Reckon we'll have an account tew settle with you, likewise, afore long!"

The talk in the sitting room went on for ten minutes longer, and then Captain Rembrandt turned suddenly to Darrel Kirk.

"Brew us up that hot drink, Kirk," he said. "I am tremendously dry."

At once the old man hurried into the kitchen and to the very pantry in which Hen was hiding. The tall Vermonter tried to drop behind a flour barrel, but his form was too elongated for this purpose and he was easily seen.

"Hen Peabody!" gasped old Kirk. "What be you a-doin' here? Hi! Hi! Here be a spy!" he bawled, as Hen

"Hen Peabody!" Gasped Old Kirk

arose and caught him by the arm, warningly.

"A spy!" exclaimed Captain Rembrandt.

"Who is it?" added Henry Windotte.

Both ran into the kitchen, each drawing a pistol as he moved. In a second more poor Hen was so well covered that escape was entirely out of the question.

"That hired man!" muttered Windotte. He remembered Hen well, having not only seen him at the Morse homestead, but also before, at the meeting in the forest, at the time of the battles of Lexington and Concord.

"Who is it?" queried the British captain.

"He is the hired man up to the house at which I am stopping. He is a great friend to that boy who spied on us up at Bedwell's house a little over a month ago."

"Indeed! And how did he come here?"

"Sure an' I don't know," put in Darrel Kirk. "All of the doors an' winders are barred, as you can easily see."

"Never mind, he is here and that is enough." Captain Rembrandt turned a fierce look upon Hen. "What have you to say for yourself, fellow?" he demanded.

"Wall, seein' ez how I'm putty well cornered, perhaps you hed better do the talkin', cap'n," drawled the Vermonter.

"You sneaked in here to spy on us."

"No; I reckon I came in tew pay Darrel Kirk a friendly

Sunday call."

"It's not so—he bees no friend to I," bawled the old man. "He bees a spy."

"Wall, ef I am it air a better business nor paradin' around in female clothes," said Hen, with a glance at Windotte.

"Your spying upon us may cost you dear, my man," said Captain Rembrandt, significantly.

"Thet's to be seen, Cap'n."

"You will see it very soon."

"Wot do ye calkerlate tew do—shoot me on the spot?"

"I don't know but what we had better."

"He ought to be shot," growled Windotte. His female attire was repulsive to him and to be twitted about it made him angry.

"If yer so cold blooded ez all thet, why, go ahead— I can't stop ye," returned the Vermonter. "But—"

"But what?"

"My friends will make ye pay the penalty, mark thet!"

"Do your friends know where you are?" asked Captain Rembrandt, quickly.

"Never mind—ye'll learn fast enough, never fear."

"Captain, the minutemen may be surrounding this house now!" burst out Henry Windotte, in alarm.

"We will soon see," was the ready reply. "Man, do

you surrender, or shall we shoot you where you stand?"

"Ef it's jest the same, I'll surrender."

"Very well. Kirk, give us a strong rope."

The article in question was quickly forthcoming, and Hen's hands and feet were tied tightly. Then he was thrown into the pantry, which had no window, and the door was closed and buttoned upon him.

"Now, Kirk, stand guard here with your gun," went on the British captain. "If he escapes it will cost you your life. Come, Windotte, perhaps we haven't a moment to spare. Fortunately I have two horses handy. Come!"

The two men ran to the front door of the house and cast open the wicket. Not a soul was in sight, and presently both emerged into the open.

"I don't see anyone, Captain."

"Nor I, Windotte; but we must be careful. You take a walk to the right and I will walk to the left. The horses are down in yonder hollow, should we need them."

Half an hour sufficed to convince the two Englishmen that nobody but Hen had come to the house. Then a consultation was had and the two went in again.

It was dark when Henry Windotte, still attired as a lady, walked back to the Morse homestead. The calculating look in his eyes was deeper than ever.

"We'll make that confounded rebel talk sooner or later," he muttered as he strode along. "He'll be mighty hungry and thirsty by tomorrow and willing to tell a thing or two for the sake of a cup of water. And if that doesn't fetch him, we can hang him up by the thumbs. That always brings them to their senses."

Reaching the house, he found that Dorothy had kept supper waiting for him and now he was hungry enough to eat a good deal, even though the Sunday fare was plain. Dorothy waited on him, at the same time wondering what had become of the hired man.

"Hen will have something to tell when he gets back, I feel certain of it," she thought. "But what can be keeping him so long? I trust no harm has befallen him."

At ten o'clock family and visitor retired. As Mrs. Morse knew nothing of Hen's disappearance, she rested in ease. But Dorothy was greatly worried and hardly closed her eyes. At five o'clock she was up and bustling around. The hired man was still absent. She went to the door of the visitor's room and listened. Not even the sound of breathing reached her ear, and after a moment's hesitation she opened the door. The room was vacant—visitor and handbag had disappeared.

CHAPTER XIII

THE TWO SPIES AND THEIR WORK

"HEN is gone?"

"Yes, Roger, he followed the woman Sunday afternoon, and that is the last I saw of him."

"And she disappeared through the night, Dorothy? Have you any idea where to?"

"None whatever. Oh, Roger, what can have become of Hen? Do you think the spies, or whatever they are, have harmed him?"

"I don't know what to think, Dorothy. Certainly something is wrong. That visitor of yours was undoubtedly the man named Windotte."

"A man!" Dorothy stood breathless for a moment. "I believe you! Oh, Roger, this is the worst of all!" and the tears started to the girl's eyes.

"No, it isn't; Hen's disappearance is the worst. But tell me all you know and I'll try to hunt him up."

Roger had come in but a few minutes before, having

ridden almost constantly since leaving Chelsea. Dick was with him, and now both dropped into chairs in the dining room, while Dorothy bustled about, preparing a warm meal for them, and telling all she knew at the same time. Mrs. Morse, quite helpless, sat in a rocking chair, looking on.

"I notified several of the men as I came along, and a strict watch will be kept for Windotte," said Roger, when his sister had finished. "But the chances are that he is safe in Boston by this time. You haven't seen anything of Deacon Marston?"

"No."

"I thought he might be around to give Windotte a hint of what has occurred. But I reckon he's so scared that he will keep out of sight, or get back to Boston as soon as he can."

"Did you notice what direction Hen took when he left?" put in Dick, who had thus far said but little.

"I think both the lady, or rather the man, and he took the Bedford road. I watched them walking past the meetinghouse."

The meal was soon dispatched, and then Roger and Dick arose.

"We must get on Hen's track," said the former. "Of course you'll help, Dick."

"To be sure, but it may be like looking for a grain of corn in a wheat bin."

"Never mind, we must find him, or find out something about him," was the determined answer. "Come, there is no use in losing any time."

"But you look ready to drop, Roger," interposed Mrs. Morse. "I dare say you have hardly slept a wink for several nights."

"That is true, Mother, but it can't be helped. I know you are as much worried about Hen as any of us."

"Yes, indeed—he has always been so faithful to our interests," and the lady of the house gave a deep sigh.

Soon Roger and Dick were off, passing the tavern and the meetinghouse, where that stirring battle had taken place only six weeks before. Then all had been bustle and excitement; now all was peaceful, the warm wind sighing through the trees and the birds singing as cheerily as if there was no such thing in life as war. But beyond the roadway the fields were still torn up from the countless tracks of men, horses, and wheels, and nothing had been done to repair the damage done to the last fall's sowing, nor had any attempt at early spring planting been made. Plowshares had been cast aside for swords and muskets, and there was no telling when the conflict was to come to an end.

Having proceeded along the Bedford road for several rods, Roger called a halt. "We won't gain anything by going it blind," he said. "Let us do a little figuring on this matter, Dick, and try to find out just where Hen went."

"I'm willing. But what can we figure on—Hen's footprints? The footprints around here all look alike to me. We might get Big Fly Charlie, the Indian, to do the tracking for us." Dick referred to a half-breed who had lived around Lexington for years. He was a splendid hunter, and as good on a trail as a bloodhound.

"I don't think the footprints will help us—there are too many of them. But if Hen came this way he was following Windotte. Now the question is, where did Windotte go?"

"I give it up, Roger."

"Below here is Mr. Bartlett's house and next comes Dickson's. Those folks we know are with us heart and soul, so it isn't likely Windotte would call upon them."

"No, he wouldn't go there."

"The next place is old Darrel Kirk's. The last time I went past, Kirk had his place entirely closed up. Would Windotte go there?"

"What for?"

"I don't know—excepting Kirk might be inclined to help the British. I always thought he was more than half a Tory."

"We can call on Kirk and see, Roger."

"Come on, then, and if we don't find anything there, let us go on to the Crandalls. Old Crandall is a Tory and getting ready to move into Boston, I know."

Off the pair set again, and ten minutes of brisk walking brought them to the maple grove in which was located Darrel Kirk's home. They had just passed the first line of trees when Dick suddenly clutched Roger's arm.

"Out of sight, quick!" he cried.

"What did you see?" asked Roger, as he dropped behind a tree stump.

"Two men just entered the back door."

"Did you recognize them?"

"No."

"Was either of them old Kirk?"

"No."

"Humph! That looks suspicious, for Kirk was never in the habit of having anybody around. He used to set that dog of his on to everyone, until Sam Dickerson up and shot the beast."

The two boys held their position behind the trees for several minutes, and then Roger motioned for Dick to follow him, and as silently as shadows the two approached close to the side of the dilapidated residence.

As before, every door and window was tightly closed below, and now those above were also fastened.

It was growing dark, and this aided them in their movements.

"I'll wager a secret meeting of some sort is going on here," whispered Roger. "Old Kirk wouldn't have everything as tight as a drum for nothing."

"You may well say as tight as a drum," grinned Dick. "Here is the airhole in the shell," and he pointed to where a pane of glass in one of the windows had a small corner broken out. Putting his ear to the opening, he listened for a moment, then motioned for Roger to do the same.

A conversation was going on inside, between three men. Roger recognized Darrel Kirk's voice, and the others sounded strangely familiar. "If I could only get a peep at them," he thought, when his eye caught sight of a round hole in one of the sackings Kirk had hung up as a substitute for a regular shade. The hole was about a foot above his head. "Lift me up, Dick, please," he whispered.

Roger's chum complied. One look into the sitting room beyond, and the minute boy was strongly tempted to give a low whistle.

"Whom did you see?" asked Dick as Roger came down.

"Kirk, that soldier named Windotte, and that Captain Rembrandt I met at Uriah Bedwell's house!" was the low but excited reply. "They are seated around the table, drinking ale and examining some papers—that is, the Britishers are examining the papers."

"Is Windotte dressed as a woman?"

"No; but there is a handbag on the floor, open, and

there is woman's clothing in it."

"Then Dorothy was right. But where is Hen?"

"That remains to be found out."

The talk had been carried on in the lowest possible whisper. Now Roger applied his ear once more to the opening.

For a long while he heard nothing that he could understand. Captain Rembrandt and Windotte were discussing figures and the movements of soldiers. Then, however, he heard something that caused him to listen more attentively than ever.

"So he won't talk yet?" said Captain Rembrandt. "He must have more backbone than I gave him credit for."

"Oh, some of these minutemen are regular oaks," returned Windotte. "A fellow must almost admire them for their sturdiness, enemies though they be."

"Bah! They are rebels, Windotte, that is enough. If I had the saying of it, I would give none of them quarter."

"He's e'enmost starved," put in Darrel Kirk, "yet he won't beg for a mouthful."

"I'll try him again," muttered Captain Rembrandt. "Remember, Windotte, we must get back to Boston tonight."

"I know it."

"If he won't talk I'll put a bullet through his head,

and we can pitch him into the pond back of here," went on the captain, determinedly, understanding full well the bold game he was playing.

He arose, and his companions followed him. Darrel Kirk, taking up the lighted candle, led the way to the cellar stairs. Down these all three went, leaving the rooms above in total darkness.

"Dick, Hen is found. He is a prisoner here, and they are starving him to death, and may shoot him!" came from Roger, in hurried tones. "We must get at him somehow."

"But how, Roger?"

"Let us try that back door. Even if it is locked we may be able to burst it open."

Away went the two lads, to find the rear door to the house latched, but the latchstring was on the outside.

Swiftly but cautiously Roger pulled upon the string, and the door came open. Then they tiptoed their way into the dark kitchen. The door to the cellar stood ajar, and from here streamed a faint light.

Both minute boys had brought their muskets along, and now they felt of the flints and locks to see if they were ready for use. Roger was the first at the head of the stairs.

"If it comes to shooting, take Windotte, the clean faced man," he whispered. "I will take care of the captain." And Dick pinched his arm to show that he understood.

"THE INHUMAN BRUTES!" THOUGHT ROGER AS HE
SURVEYED THE SCENE

They listened intently, then moved like shadows down the steps. Looking ahead, they saw that Hen had been tied to a beam in the front part of the cellar. Each thumb had a rope around it, and his body was hoisted up so that just his toes touched the stone flooring.

"The inhuman brutes!" thought Roger, as he surveyed the scene. He was tempted to put a bullet through the British Captain on the spot.

"No, I won't tell ye nuthin'," Hen was saying. "I'm done with ye."

"Don't you care to live?" demanded Captain Rembrandt.

"Not at the price ye ask. If ye think tew murder me, do so an' hev done with it."

"You had better tell our captain what you know," put in Windotte.

"I've said all I'm a-goin' tew say. I hate the sight o' a redcoat an' a Tory, an' thet's enough."

Hen's coolness seemed to exasperate Captain Rembrandt beyond all endurance. He was naturally a hot-tempered man, and now he lost complete control of himself.

"I won't bother with him, Windotte!" he cried, passionately. "He is a rebel and a traitor to our good King George III, and as such I shall shoot him down where he stands, and feel justified in doing it. Man, if you have any prayers to say, say them now; for in two minutes you shall die."

As he concluded, Captain Rembrandt pulled out his pistol and aimed it squarely at the Vermonter's heart. For once in his life Hen Peabody turned pale; for it looked to him as if his last moment on earth had come, and that nothing could interfere to save him.

CHAPTER XIV

OFF FOR THE FRONT

"STOP!"

The unexpected command, coming from directly behind them, caused Captain Rembrandt and Windotte to wheel around swiftly.

"Who spoke?" questioned the captain, as soon as he could catch his breath.

"I did," came from behind the cellar stairs, and now the British captain saw a musket barrel protruding from a hole in the back boarding of the fifth step. "Drop that pistol, or you're a dead man."

"We are discovered!" gasped Darrel Kirk. "Oh, what shall I do!" and he fell upon his knees.

"The Old Nick take the luck!" burst from Windotte. "Come on, Captain, there is no time to—"

The crack of a musket swallowed up the remainder of his speech. Captain Rembrandt, instead of dropping his weapon, had turned it toward the steps. It was

Roger's firearm that spoke up, and down went the British officer's arm to his side, while the pistol clanked on the stones.

"Stand where you are, both of you," came from Dick, and now those in the front of the cellar saw one musket barrel withdrawn and another hastily substituted. The boys were safe behind the broad steps, and could fire from the hole as from the port of a fortress.

"Don't shoot!" screamed Darrel Kirk. "I surrender! Don't shoot, for the love of heaven!"

"Don't shoot!" added Windotte, likewise much alarmed, as he saw the captain's arm go down. In the meantime Roger was reloading with all possible speed.

"Heaven be praised!" came from Hen. "Shoot 'em down, men, shoot 'em down! They desarve it!" he went on, thinking some men of Lexington had come to his rescue.

"Stand perfectly still!" went on Dick. "A single step and I'll fire!"

"Oh, spare an old man, an' take all I have!" came, with a groan, from old Kirk.

By this time Roger's musket was again ready for use; and now he stepped from behind the stairs, leaving Dick still at the hole.

"Roger!" exclaimed Hen, in glad surprise.

"Captain Rembrandt, don't move," said the youth. "Darrel Kirk, listen to me. You undoubtedly have a knife in your pocket. Take it out and cut the ropes that bind Hen Peabody. Windotte, a single step will cost you your life."

"I—I'll do any—anything!" gasped Darrel Kirk. "Only don't—don't shoot!"

Trembling in every limb, the old man succeeded, after some trouble, in producing his jackknife; and going up to Hen, he cut the Vermonter down, and then cut the ropes from his wrists and his ankles.

The instant Hen was released, he ran forward and caught up Captain Rembrandt's pistol. In the meantime, Kirk ran to a far corner and crouched down in a heap. The old man was now so completely overcome that he was losing his wits.

"Hen, supposing you bind our prisoners?" suggested Roger. "Turn about is fair play."

"Gosh! But thet's a capital idee," chuckled the Vermonter. He caught up the rope and approached Windotte. "I hain't forgot you," he said. "Remember when you an' thet tudder crowd was a-goin' tew burn me with a red hot bayonet? I reckon the boot is on tudder leg, now, eh?"

Windotte turned pale, and gave a shiver. Yes, he remembered only too well, and he felt that he could expect no mercy at the tall Yankee's hands.

But now there came a swift and unexpected change. Without being noticed, Captain Rembrandt had moved a little nearer to the candle, which stood in its candlestick on a keg. A swift blow, and out went the light, leaving the cellar in total darkness.

Three shots rang out, coming from the two boys and Hen, and a yell from Windotte followed. Then came a rush for the cellar stairs, and three or four met in a bunch there and went down.

"Who is this?" cried Dick, grabbing somebody by the arm. "Speak up!"

"It's me!" came from Hen, and the two separated. In the meantime, Roger had caught hold of Windotte, who was shot through the shoulder. But somebody had gone up the steps three at a time, and was now making for the cottage door. It was Captain Rembrandt.

As quickly as it could be done a light was struck, and the candle relit. It was found that Windotte was out of the struggle, having fainted from pain and the loss of blood. Darrel Kirk remained in his corner, shrieking loudly that he be spared, even if they took all he possessed.

"The captain—?" began Roger.

"He went up," answered Dick. "He hit me here," and he pointed to his left cheek, which was bleeding from a scratching blow.

"Dick, stay here an' take charge," put in Hen. "Come on, Roger," and away he went up the cellar stairs, with the boy close behind him.

But to make a light and understand the situation had taken time, and now, as they emerged into the open air, they heard Captain Rembrandt urging forward his horse, which had been tethered in the woods behind the dwelling. "Go, Lionel, go!" came loudly. "Go, as you never went before, for my life depends upon it!" and then there was a flash of man and horseflesh, as both disappeared down a trail leading to the Boston highway.

Hen and Roger fired, but missed their mark. Then each looked inquiringly at the other.

"He's got the best of it, so far," said Roger. "If we had horses—"

"Hain't thar another hoss around—one belongin' tew Windotte?" questioned the Vermonter.

"That's so! Come and look."

They started immediately, but in five minutes felt assured that, if there had been such an animal, Captain Rembrandt had driven it off before mounting his own.

Feeling that pursuit on foot would be useless, both returned to Darrel Kirk's house, to find that Dick and Kirk had carried Windotte upstairs and laid him on a couch. The Britisher was just coming to his senses.

"Spare an old man," began Kirk, on seeing them, and fell upon his knees. "Don't give me up to the— the mob!" He was filled with terror, for he remembered well how an old man of Salem, also a traitor, had been ridden through the town on a wooden horse, and had been smeared in tar and rolled in feathers, after which he was driven into the woods and threatened with shooting on sight. What became of this individual was never afterward ascertained.

"Is he badly hurt?" asked Roger, ignoring the old fellow.

"I think he is."

"Then we must get a doctor for him."

The matter was talked over, and it was decided that Dick should go for Doctor Hardwaithe; Hen, who was still sore, should remain with the wounded man, and Roger should follow up Captain Rembrandt's trail.

Roger felt certain that, now he had been discovered, the British captain would make straight for Charlestown or Boston Neck. He ran down the road to Lexington Green, told half a dozen men of what had occurred, and then sped over home, where he procured a farm horse, mounting the animal with only a potato sack for a saddle.

The hunt lasted far into the night, but was unsuccessful. Captain Rembrandt was shrewd enough to keep out of sight as much as possible, and passed into Boston by way of the Neck the next morning at four o'clock, having bribed a guard who was already half Tory. It may be as well to add here that Deacon Marston also managed to get into the besieged town.

On the following Saturday, Windotte, still suffering a good deal, was transferred to the British hospital at West Cambridge, from which, later on, he was removed to Boston, having first sworn to keep silent concerning all he might have learned about the Continental army and its proposed movements. To Windotte's credit, it must be recorded that for once he kept his word. His wound did not heal rapidly, and in the middle of the summer he was returned to England in a relief ship and discharged from the king's service on a pension.

Darrel Kirk was thought to be too old to be punished. Yet there were those in Lexington and vicinity who had not forgotten his quarrelsome manner in his younger days, and one night they surrounded his home, dragged him forth, and threw him into a mud hole down by the brook. His cries for mercy were received with jeers, and he was told to pack up his belongings and move inside of twenty-four hours. He did so, going to a sister who lived at Acton, where, all crippled up with rheumatism, he lived to become an even hundred years old and then died.

It may well be believed that both Roger and Hen were worn out when they returned to the Morse homestead. Roger was so sleepy he could scarcely keep his eyes open, and the hired man was hungry to the last degree. But food and rest could now be had in plenty, and by the opening of the first week in June boy and man felt as well as ever.

Many of the minutemen and boys who had driven the British into Boston had come home on furloughs, their places being taken by the fresh troops which were arriving almost daily. But during the middle of the next week it was rumored that the enemy was planning some sort of sally from Boston, and the order came that all who were able should again present themselves at the front.

"That means us," said Roger to Hen. "Of course you'll go."

"Shall you go?" asked Mrs. Morse, anxiously. Roger looked at his fond parent earnestly. "Mother, if my country needs me, would you have me stay away?" he said.

"No, my son; do your duty. But, oh, be careful, for I—I cannot spare you and your father, too!"

And so it was decided that Roger should leave home on the following morning. Dick, Paul, Ben and all of the other minute boys were also going. Mrs. Morse told Hen he could go likewise, to keep an eye on Roger, just as the faithful man had done at the battles of Lexington and Concord.

It was a warm, misty day when the crowd started, eighteen strong, counting all of the boys, as well as the old soldiers. Each was armed with a new musket, taken from the lot unearthed at Uriah Bedwell's house, and each carried likewise sixteen rounds of ammunition. All were on foot, excepting a certain Lieutenant Dangerfield, who had come over from New Hampshire, and who accompanied them as far as Charlestown Common, the wide stretch of meadowland to the west of Charlestown Neck.

A crowd had gathered to see them march away, without a drum it is true, but with everybody cheering, and with hats and handkerchiefs waving.

"Good-bye, boys. God go with you, and bring you success!" was heard coming from more than one good dame or old man. The smaller inhabitants yelled and whistled, while up at the tavern some of those who had been wounded and could not go fired a salute from several muskets.

As they passed the homestead, Roger looked back, and so did Hen, and took off their hats. Mrs. Morse and Dorothy stood by the gate, both with their handkerchiefs to their eyes. To them this parting was a sad one. Mrs. Morse spoke the sentiment that was in the heart of each. "Roger is so young," she sobbed. "Only a boy! Oh, I trust he returns to us alive and well."

Dorothy said nothing, but strained her eyes to watch the soldiers, until at last a turn in the highway hid them from view. Then mother and daughter went into the house. It was to be many days and weeks before either was to see Roger again.

CHAPTER XV

Working on Breed's Hill Breastworks

General Gage, finding himself penned in Boston, resolved to do two things without delay—declare martial law, and fortify the Heights of Dorchester, a strategic point of land south of Boston proper. Reinforcements were coming in, and he felt that the rebellion must be crushed without further delay.

The document declaring martial law was very arrogantly worded, and angered the colonists greatly. The latter were spoken of as rebels and traitors, and were called upon to throw down their arms and submit to royal authority without further discussion. If this was done, all might hope for forgiveness, excepting John Hancock and Samuel Adams, who were put down as ringleaders, and who must submit to condign punishment. General Gage would have been much better off had that document never been penned, for had such been the case it is barely possible that peace might have been patched up, even though blood upon both sides had already been shed.

As the Americans paid no attention to his paper further than to sneer and jeer at it, he set about fortifying Dorchester Heights, and also spoke of taking possession of Bunker and Breed's Hills, then commonly known as Charlestown Heights. In the meantime, General Burgoyne and other military officers arrived, to take active charge of the British forces. General Burgoyne's manner was even worse than that of General Gage. On arriving he demanded to know how affairs stood, and was told that there were about ten thousand colonists besieging the town.

"And how many troops have we?" he continued.

"About five thousand at present that are fit for regular service."

"What! Five thousand soldiers of our king being shut up by ten thousand miserable peasants!" stormed Burgoyne. "Well, let us in and we will soon find elbowroom." He came in, but "elbowroom" was not so easily gained, as Burgoyne soon discovered, much to his chagrin. From the way the British general used the term, "elbowroom" became a common saying throughout the entire Revolution in speaking of the troubles at Boston, New York, Philadelphia, and other cities which the British were forced to abandon.

The news that the enemy were about to move upon

Dorchester and Charlestown Heights reached the American camp, and it was this which caused those on furlough to be called again to the front. What was going to be done was not definitely known, and the American army rested on its guns with great anxiety, looking for an attack at any moment.

The colonial committee of safety and the council of war held a meeting, and a committee was appointed to see what was best to be done. The committee recommended that breastworks and redoubts be constructed at Prospect Hill, Winter Hill, Bunker Hill, and several other points. So far the only fortifications erected by the Americans had been a small earthworks at Cambridge.

Gage had fixed upon the night of June the eighteenth to advance upon Dorchester Heights and take possession. News of this intended movement reached the American camp five or six days before. Immediately all the regiments were ordered to hold themselves in readiness to march or to fight, as occasion might require. Then came a secret order to fortify Bunker Hill without further delay, "with men sufficient to hold it, and with large cannon, to sweep the bay upon both sides."

Charlestown, at this period, was a peninsula about a mile long and half a mile wide, lying nearly to the north of Boston. On the eastern shore the Medford, or Mystic, River came down into the harbor, and on the western side was the Charles River. The shape of the peninsula was not unlike a fat pear, and the stem would represent the Neck, to the northwest, where it was joined to the mainland at the Common, previously mentioned. The land at the Neck was low and at very high tides was completely submerged.

The town of Charlestown lay directly opposite Boston, on the southern slope of the peninsula. To the north were several rises of ground, that on the eastern extremity being known as Moulton's Point, followed by Breed's Hill, seventy-five feet high, and Bunker Hill, a hundred and ten feet high. On the northeast side of the hills the ground was clayey and full of dangerous waterholes, and was used for nothing but clay pits and brick kilns. On the southwestern slope were pastures and rich orchards, and through these ran Main Street, running from the ferry in Charlestown to the Neck and having upon it a handful of houses and scattered places of business. Charlestown proper numbered several hundred homes.

The expedition to Bunker Hill was placed under the command of Colonel William Prescott, and numbered about twelve hundred men. It was gathered upon Cambridge Common, portions of several different commands being selected for the work. At first the minute boys of Lexington were afraid they would be left behind, but at the last moment one of the captains came along and said they might take part, if they did not think the risk was too great.

"We are to work as secretly as possible," he said. "If the enemy discover us we may be killed to a man."

"I am willing to take the risk," said Roger. "I came to the front to do or die for our colonies, as Heaven may see best." Of course the faithful Hen went with "his boys," as he now termed them.

It was evening when the command assembled upon Cambridge Common. All felt the responsibility of the undertaking, and the worthy president of Harvard College was asked to address the soldiers and pray for them, which he did most fervently.

"Forward march!" came the command, at nine o'clock, and silently the companies moved forward for Charlestown Neck, two sergeants with dark lanterns at the head, to give warning if any pitfalls appeared. Behind the sergeants came Colonel Prescott, modestly arrayed in a blue coat and three cornered hat. Regulation uniforms for officers and men were not forthcoming for our entire army until Washington took command and began his work of reorganization.

"We're off at last!" whispered Dick to Roger.

"I think we'll see some fun before we get back."

"Perhaps we'll see more than we wish, Dick," was the grim response. "Remember, this is no merrymaking party."

"This is an uncommonly heavy load to carry," put in Ben Small, who was struggling along with his musket over one shoulder and a crowbar and a pick over the other.

"Don't worry, Ben," said Roger. "I am no better off, with this spade, which I'll warrant is twice as heavy as any we've got at home."

"It would be all right if our muskets weren't so awfully heavy," put in Dick. "This new one weighs exactly nineteen pounds. I understand the Tower guns the British have weigh only fourteen or fifteen pounds."

"Some of 'em air even lighter," came from Hen, who strode along with musket, spade, and several other things useful for entrenching. "But look here, lads, ef any of ye air sick o' this undertakin' why don't ye quit right now? I reckon the colonel will let ye off, seein' ez how ye ain't none o' ye o' age, and—"

"Back out!" came from all. "Not much, Hen! We're in this to stay!" and that was the last of the grumbling. At the Neck several carts came up, and the tools were thrown into these, much to the lads' relief.

"Now, men, all of you must remain strictly silent," came the order. "If anything must be said, say it in a whisper, for the British spies are everywhere. Picket guards will be thrown out, and if an alarm comes, drop whatever tools you may have in hand and form in company ranks with your muskets."

Following instructions, Captain Nutting with his men was ordered down Main Street to the town proper as a guard. Then the regular body of the troops took their way up the road leading to the top of Bunker Hill. The way was dark and uncertain, and all had to move with caution, for fear of falling into some ambush; for since the Americans had heard of Gage's plans, all argued that the British might likewise have heard of what they were going to do.

"There may be two or three thousand redcoats waiting for us up there," said one officer, pointing along the hill slopes. "Have your flints ready, boys."

Yet that night but one alarm came, and that of no importance, as was afterward ascertained. A man was found lying behind a tree and was taken to be a spy. When discovered, he acted as if he were intoxicated. The officers would not believe this, shook him vigorously, and at last gave him a pailful of cold water over his head. This revived the fellow a bit, and he told where he belonged in Charlestown. The case was investigated and it was learned that the man was a confirmed drunkard, and harmless.

At last the top of Bunker Hill was gained, and here a halt was called. The chief engineer of the party was Colonel Gridley, a veteran of much experience. The ground was looked over, and Gridley came to the conclusion that it would be better to place the outworks on Breed's Hill, somewhat closer to Boston.

"But the main work must be at Bunker Hill," said another of the party. "That is the instructions."

A long discussion followed, but in the end the first redoubt was placed on the slope of Breed's Hill, within twelve hundred yards of the Boston batteries and still closer to the *Lively, Falcon, Somerset,* and other British war vessels lying in the harbor.

"To work, lads, and waste not a moment," cried Colonel Prescott, after the engineering corps had staked out the ground and explained just what was to be done.

"We'll dig as we never dug before!" cried Sandy Beane, a well digger from Connecticut, who had been placed in charge of one of the entrenching parties. "Along this line first, men, and then that line, and heap the dirt up well along this bank. We'll make a breastworks the redcoats will have a fine shindy getting to," and down came Beane's pick; and the work started.

With so many hands, and among boys and men who had used picks and shovels from childhood, the work advanced rapidly. The officers stalked around here and there, with their lanterns, watching the proceedings and giving directions, and some even went to work themselves in the trenches. Colonel Prescott, expecting hot work, wore a linen frock, in place of his former blue coat, and daylight found him still with this linen outfit, worn all through the famous battle now so close at hand.

The protection for the soldiers consisted of a redoubt about eight rods square, and a breastworks over four hundred feet long, the former facing Main Street and the latter running over the slopes toward the Mystic River. It was the intention to make the breastworks longer, but the coming of daylight brought the labors of the soldiers to an end.

That night in the trenches was one Roger never forgot. Working like a beaver in silence, with guns close at hand, the men threw up dirt and stones, and packed them down. It was a clear starlit night, and it seemed impossible that the British would not discover what was going on. Down by the water's edge, the warships were almost in sight, and from the British guard on the Charlestown shore Colonel Prescott heard the cry, "All's well" as fresh pickets came on to relieve the old.

Four o'clock came, and now in the east could be seen the first faint light of the coming sun. "We'll have to quit soon!" was the word passed around, but still the soldiers kept at work, putting the finishing touches to this point and that. They had had a single ration dealt out to them on leaving Cambridge, and now this was hastily dispatched, along with large quantities of water, for the coming day promised to be exceedingly warm.

At last the sun came up, and to the astonished gaze of the British, they saw the American defenses reared up proudly where the day before only peaceful pastures had lain. For awhile they could not believe their eyesight. There must be some mistake, they told each other. Would those rebels and traitors dare to be so bold?

The first discovery of the entrenchments was made by a watcher on the British ship *Lively,* that lay but a short distance off the Charlestown shore. At once all was hubbub and excitement. The captain of the vessel came on deck and took in the situation in speechless amazement, then ordered a broadside to be fired at the workers that still remained in view. The broadside was speedily forthcoming, and this was really the opening of the famous battle of Bunker Hill.

CHAPTER XVI

The Bombardment from the Warships

Boom!

Loud and clear over the waters of the harbor, over Boston itself, and over the outlying territory rang the first broadside of the *Lively,* sending a rain of lead before and over the American defenses.

"We're discovered now, thet's sartin!" burst out Hen, as he dropped the shovel with which he had been working and seized his musket. "Gosh all hemlock, listen tew thet!"

Again came a broadside, speedily taken up by the *Falcon*, *Somerset*, and other vessels, and from a battery on Copp's Hill in Boston. Spop! The cannonballs hit the earthworks and sank out of sight. Spop! Spop! They kept coming on steadily.

"They have our range!" exclaimed Roger, who had also picked up his musket. "They can reach us even if we can't reach them—yet."

"Don't leave the work, boys!" came the cry. "We must finish before they send on an attacking party. Be careful of what you do, but don't tarry in your labors."

At first the men had been dismayed, but now, the first excitement over, they stacked their weapons once more and seized their tools. Soon the work on the defenses was going on as calmly as though the shades of night were still protecting them. But it was hot work, for the sun had come up clear and strong, and all dripped with perspiration.

"I'm not afraid of 'em," cried a soldier from Billerica named Asa Pollard. "I'll go outside and finish up," and he leaped over the earthworks at a single bound.

"Better come back here," roared Hen. "There might something hap—"

Another broadside from one of the war vessels swallowed up the remainder of his speech. Spop! Spop! Came the balls. Then followed a silence.

"How do ye like thet, Pollard?" cried a fellow soldier standing beside Roger. No reply came back, and the man stretched up to look over the breastworks. Then he gave a hoarse yell. "He's dead! He's dead!"

Instantly a score mounted the breastworks, forgetting all about their own danger. Yes, Pollard was dead, a cannonball having mangled him frightfully. Soon the report circulated, and those who had exposed themselves ran hastily for shelter.

"It's tew bad," said Hen, his honest face full of sorrow. "Poor Pollard, the fust tew go down. Wall, I reckon he won't be the last, not by a good many. I feel it in my bones thet we have a bloody day's work afore us."

Pollard was well-beloved by the other members of Stickney's company, to which he belonged, and his friends insisted on taking his body in and giving it a decent burial.

"But we haven't time for any religious services," said some of the officers.

"Then we'll take time," was the reply of those men whose faith was uppermost even in these hours of peril. A clergyman, the Reverend John Martin, was present, and he performed the burial ceremony while several hundred looked on. Later in the day this same clergyman threw aside his church dignity, buckled on a sword, and fought as bravely as anybody.

The taking off of Asa Pollard made some of the volunteers falter, especially those who had taken no part in the battles of Lexington and Concord, and had heretofore seen no bloodshed. Some were for retiring, but the others urged them to remain.

"Don't turn tail, boys, don't!" came the cry. "We'll wax old Gage, never fear!"

Seeing how affairs were turning, Colonel Prescott threw off his three-cornered hat and bareheaded, mounted to the top of the earthworks, sword in hand.

"Fellow soldiers, we came here to show the British what we intend to do," he said. "Here we remain. We are safe, and a most glorious victory awaits us. I will lead you, no matter what comes. Won't you follow me?"

"We will! We will! Hurrah for Prescott!" came the rallying cry, and those on the point of departing turned back; and the work on the defenses was renewed.

Colonel Prescott's bravery in thus showing himself brought about a very curious result. In Boston, General Gage had taken himself to a hill and was viewing the scene through a telescope, while a dozen others stood silently by wondering what the commander would do.

"Who is that officer commanding?" demanded the general, handing his glass to one of the gentlemen, a lawyer named Willard. The lawyer gave a careful look.

"That, sir, is my brother-in-law, Colonel Prescott," was the astonishing reply.

"Indeed!" cried Gage. "And will he fight?"

"Yes, sir, depend upon it, to the last drop of blood in him."

"And what of the men under him?" continued the discomfited British commander.

"I cannot answer for his men," was the guarded answer; but Willard knew that the minutemen would fight to the bitter end. General Gage turned away, shaking his head doubtfully.

Without delay the British held a council of war. The Americans had stolen a march upon them, and should they be permitted to fortify Breed's Hill and Bunker Hill with cannon, Boston would be completely at their mercy. "We must send them a-flying," was the general conclusion reached. But how? was the all important question. Many remembered the disaster attendant upon the expedition to Concord only too well, and felt they must be cautious.

A number of the officers voted to take a strong command to Charlestown Neck and effect a landing under the protection of the warships and floating batteries. This done, they would drive the enemy from the rear into Charlestown or over to Moulton's Point, and there compel them to surrender or cut them to pieces.

But Gage overruled this plan. "*They* may do a little of the driving," said he. "And if so, our soldiers will be caught between those now on Bunker Hill and those who may put in a forced march from Cambridge. If our companies be caught on the Neck, nothing can save them from being either shot or drowned."

And so it was decided that the American forces should be attacked from the front, the landing of the British soldiers to take place as soon as possible on and around Moulton Point. Without delay the *Falcon* was sent around to the Point to clear it with grape,

COLONEL PRESCOTT MOUNTED TO THE TOP OF THE
EARTHWORKS, SWORD IN HAND

round, and chain shot.

On Bunker and Breed's Hills the work was not yet finished. In several spots were rail fences, and one of these was pulled up and piled against another, and over the whole was packed a lot of hay which lay in some of the pastures drying. Some of my young readers may laugh at such a defense, but let me state that oftimes a soft substance like hay will stop a bullet or a cannonball which would easily pierce something harder. In the great Civil War, bales of cotton were found to be better in many cases than blocks of granite would have been.

The sun was now scorching and water was scarce. Many of the soldiers, who had come in from a long distance, and who had worked all through the night, could scarcely keep their eyes open.

"We must have water, food, and reinforcements," said Colonel Prescott, and sent off for them. General Putnam also demanded that additional troops be forthcoming.

But General Ward hesitated about sending more soldiers over the Neck, fearing he would weaken the guard held back to defend Cambridge and Watertown. "All of our scanty military stores are housed at those points," he declared. "What if Gage should not attack Bunker Hill at all, but come over directly to the mainland?" However, at eleven o'clock General Ward changed his

mind, and sent over the New Hampshire troops, under
Colonels Reed and Stark. Each man of these companies
received two flints, a gill of powder, and fifteen balls,
the latter of various sizes, so that the soldiers had to
beat them into shape to fit the caliber of their guns
when putting up their homemade cartridges. What a
difference between such rude supplies and those dealt
out to the soldier of today!

Slowly the forenoon wore away on Breed's Hill. Some
soldiers had been sent back to begin the work on Bunker
Hill proper, but our minute boys and Hen were not
among them. A few rations and some water was supplied
and disappeared like magic. Roger, Dick, and their
friends were "dead played out," as Ben put it, but the
excitement kept them wide awake. At last the
reinforcements were seen approaching, and a cheer
went up.

The cannonading now became more terrific than
ever, a flood tide having enabled the British to float
several batteries close to the Charlestown shore. This
terrorized the few inhabitants remaining in town and
they fled, leaving not a soul in the place. At the same
time the minutemen sent down Main Street joined the
other American forces.

"Will they attack us?" Such was the question asked
a hundred times during that hot June morning. With
their telescopes, the officers could plainly see the British

soldiers, on foot and on horseback, marching around the streets of Boston. In the meantime many barges were being collected at Long Wharf and at the North Battery. This showed that the redcoats were coming out. But to where?

"Ef they come here, we'll have our hands full, b'gosh!" observed Hen, who was building a platform of stones, upon which the minute boys might stand and fire at the enemy should an engagement come. "But ef they move over to Cambridge or Chelsea then I reckon sum other folks will have their hands full. I must confess I'm gittin' mighty anxious."

The anxiety was shared by Colonel Prescott, General Putnam, and General Warren, who had arisen from his bed suffering from a nervous headache. The worthy doctor was urged not to expose himself at Bunker Hill, but he answered that he felt it his duty to go to the front, come what might. And to the front he went, where he was immediately recognized as the leader, although he refused to take the military command from Prescott. As to who actually led on that memorable day, it may be as well to let the matter rest by stating that all of the officers worked together, and that Warren's glory, great as it was, hardly outshines that of Prescott, Putnam, and a dozen others; nor does it outshine the glories due the militia and the minute boys and men, who fought as only those can fight whose hearts and souls are in the battle.

At last came a cry that aroused everybody. "They are putting off! The British are embarking!" In a trice every man and boy was striving to gain some point from which to get a good view. "Are they moving yet? Which way are they heading?"

Then came a few more minutes of suspense. The barges at Long Wharf were filling slowly, but at last they were full, and the first of them shot out into the harbor and into the strong sunlight, that reflected vividly the scarlet uniforms, the shining muskets and the glittering bayonets. Slowly the boats moved on with their living freight, slowly and cautiously up past the North Battery and the shipyards. They then headed straight for Moulton's Point. Now the suspense ended, and those on the hills behind Charlestown knew that a bloody battle was but a question of a few hours.

CHAPTER XVII

The Opening of the Battle of Bunker Hill

"They are coming over here, Dick!"

"So they are, Roger—and that means warm work for us."

"Warm work!" broke in Paul Darly. "Great Christopher Columbus! It's warm enough up here without doing anything. I'd give two shillings for an ice cold drink from our well at home."

"Don't mention it," exclaimed Ben. "But when we get to fighting I reckon we'll forget all about feeling dry or being hungry."

He had scarcely spoken when the cannonading from the British ships, which had slackened up, broke out again, and grape shot raked Moulton's Point and Morton's Hill, a slight eminence behind it.

"Thirty-two barges full of soldiers," cried an officer, who had a glass, "and the leading boats mount several guns."

"Why don't the reinforcements come," growled another. "Are we to be left here all alone to be slain?"

"Slain?" shouted Colonel Prescott, who overheard the remark. "Don't think of it, man. We have the best of it, and if they dare to approach this hill they will suffer bitter defeat. The reinforcements will arrive in due time. Doctor Warren has promised them within twenty minutes." This was true, the zealous doctor had promised the soldiers, but he could not move the regiments alone, and through various delays and mistakes, a large number of the reinforcements failed to arrive in time to do much good.

General Howe was in command of the attacking party, which numbered about two thousand grenadiers and light infantry and a small force of artillery. The men carried several days' rations and were heavily loaded with their outfits, these outfits in some instances weighing a hundred pounds! The folly of making men carry such loads in hot weather showed itself fully before the fiery sun went down.

The embarkation had taken place about noon, and at one o'clock the first of the barges landed at Moulton's Point, now occupied by the Boston Navy Yard, and the redcoats came ashore and planted their artillery to the best advantage. Forming his command into three lines, General Howe reconnoitered the American position.

"It is strong—we need more men before we can

take it," he said, and immediately sent back to Gage for additional troops.

The American troops could do nothing, their cannon being still on the other side of Bunker Hill, to prevent a possible landing on the north shore. From their breastworks they viewed the landing in silence, but held their muskets in readiness to use the moment the enemy came close enough.

"Wall, ef thet ain't gall!" burst from Hen, presently. "By gum! ef only I had a cannon here now!"

"What is wrong?" questioned Roger.

"Them boats is goin' back, an' hang me ef them air Britishers ain't squattin' in the grass and eatin' their dinners, an' us poor hungry mortals ain't got a mouthful!" Hen's report was true. The redcoats were taking advantage of the halt to dine—to many a poor fellow his last meal on earth.

Slowly the minutes passed from one to three o'clock, and still the British troops rested where they had landed. But now their reinforcements put into appearance, landing and moving straight for the redoubt. Various authorities state the soldiers to have numbered from twenty-eight to thirty-two hundred.

The firing from the British ships of war was now heavier than ever, it being intended that this should cover up the advance of the grenadiers and light infantry. The fieldpieces also spoke up, and our artillery replied

as best it could, which was but feebly. Several times
the American cannons were changed from one position
to another, but the service rendered, meant to be well,
amounted to but little, for powder and ball were scarce,
and trained gunners were even scarcer.

"They are coming!" Such was the cry which rang
throughout the American line stretching from the redoubt
to the breastworks and on to the rail fence. It was
true, the redcoats were coming forward in two wings,
the right under General Howe to pierce the colonists'
line at the rail fence, and the left, under General Pigot,
to assault the breastworks and the redoubt.

The oncoming was certainly calculated to cause
the raw American troops to falter. Here was company
after company of well-trained soldiery marching forward
swiftly, regardless of the heavy outfits and the boiling
hot sun. Each shining Tower musket could be distinctly
seen, and the ugly looking bayonets were enough to
cause many a heart to shudder. "We can't stand against
'em," muttered more than one minuteman. "We must!"
was the invariable answer. "Remember Lexington and
Concord, and give it to 'em hot!"

General Putnam was now in his element, and tore
around on his horse, here, there, and everywhere.
"Powder is scarce and must not be wasted," he cried
out. "Don't fire at the enemy until you can see the
whites of their eyes. Fire low, take aim at their waistbands.

You are all marksmen who can hit a squirrel at a hundred yards; reserve your fire and the enemy will be destroyed. Aim at the handsome coats, pick off the commanders."

"We will! We will! Hurrah fer Old Put!" came the answering cry. Putnam's orders were repeated by Prescott, Pomeroy, Reed, and others who understood their value, and as a consequence, although a few sharpshooters could not resist the temptation to shoot as soon as the British came into range, the majority waited until their aim could become a certainty.

"Now fer it, boys, do yer duty, every mother's son on ye!" yelled Hen, who stood up between Roger and Dick. "Air yer muskets all right?"

"Mine is," said Roger. He was almost too excited to speak.

"So is mine," came from Dick, and the others also answered in the affirmative.

Up and up came the long British line, scarlet and steel flashing defiantly, the tall hats of the grenadiers coming closer and closer. Here and there from the American lines a musket shot rang out, but otherwise there was almost a deathlike silence. Roger's heart was in his throat, and beat like a trip-hammer. Former contests had been bad enough, yet it needed no experienced eye to tell that that which was to come would be infinitely worse.

"Remember, the whites of their eyes!" cried the

captain in command. "Aim low, make every bullet tell. Pick off the man straight ahead of you, and let your neighbor take the next fellow. All ready now—wait—wait—steady now, steady. Now, then—give it to 'em!"

Crack! Spat! Crack! Bang! Spoke up the muskets of the hasty ones, and then followed a long, sullen rattle and a roar, as the first line opened fire. With them the officers also fired, each of them having picked up a musket somewhere.

When the thick smoke cleared away; the effect of that opening volley was seen in all of its horror. Nearly the entire front rank of the British had been cut down, and the dead and dying lay in every direction.

"I brought him down," muttered Hen. "I knew I could do it! Will call us rebels, eh? Well, mebbe, an' glad of it, b'gosh!" The tall Vermonter had aimed at a leading officer, and his messenger of death had reached its mark.

Not far away stood a sharpshooter on a small wooden stand which he and others had built. He was the best marksman along the breastworks, and as soon as he had discharged one musket another was handed to him. In this manner he succeeded in bringing down a dozen or more British leaders. But some equally good marksman of the Royal Welsh Fusileers saw him, and laid him low without warning.

The enemy had to climb over numerous fences,

for both Bunker and Breed's Hills were cut up into pasture lots, owned by the householders of Charlestown. These, added to their heavy burdens, made their progress slow, and now that galling first fire caused them to pause. Of course they fired in return, but the Americans were well-protected, and hardly a man was injured.

A second rush was now made, and then another and another. But the success at the opening stimulated the Americans, and growing bolder, they appeared at the level of the breastworks, and sent in volley after volley, against which the British found it impossible to stand. A company would come up, only to lose a half or three quarters of their men. "We cannot take the works—it is a sheer impossibility," cried some of the underofficers, and at last General Pigot was forced to withdraw his wing out of gunshot.

A wild cheering went up. "They are retreating! They are retreating!" Then Yankee Doodle burst forth with vigor. In the past the English had tantalized the colonists with that air; now it was hurled back at them in defiance, and was henceforth to become what it is to us all today.

The other wing of the enemy was also demoralized for the time being, and Howe withdrew to join Pigot, and rearrange his plans. This gave the Americans a breathing spell, of which they were glad to avail themselves.

"Look, look!" cried Roger, as he gazed toward

Charlestown. "What a black smoke!"

"The town is on fire!" came the cry from another quarter. "See, half a dozen houses are in flames."

"And so is the church," put in Dick, as the flames suddenly burst forth from the tall steeple. "That is too bad!"

"Who knows but what Boston will go down before this battle is over!" said Paul. "When a fight begins, there is no telling when it will end."

All watched the progress of the conflagration with interest. It had been started from a carcass thrown from one of the warships. This set fire to a barn, a second caught on a house, and in five minutes the wind had done its work in the deserted town, although presently a party from the *Somerset* came ashore to finish the destruction.

As the flames mounted higher and higher, so did the indignation of the colonists. "If they cannot capture, they intend to destroy!" was the thought that ran around, and General Putnam and others rushed off upon horseback to hurry along the reinforcements. Some of these oncoming troops were found bunched on Charlestown Common, afraid to pass the Neck, which was being swept by a heavy fire from the frigate *Glasgow*. In vain Putnam rode back and forth on the neck to show how they could pass unharmed. "You're bulletproof, general," was the cry. "We ain't, nohow!" The firing at the Neck grew heavier, and only a small portion of the foot soldiery ventured across. One company tried to build a raft to float on the north side of the causeway, but this went to pieces, leaving some thirty men floundering in the mud.

The sun still poured down hotly and the air was suffocating. "Water, give us water if you want us to fight!" was the appeal, but water was scarce, and when a pailful came up, it had to do for an entire company. In the meantime the wounded were carried back and cared for as tenderly as circumstances permitted. Thus far all of the minute boys had escaped injury, although one lad had sprained his ankle through slipping from a heap of stones while firing his heavy musket.

Down in front of the defenses the scene was truly horrible. In the glare of the afternoon sun lay the British dead, with the wounded and dying crawling over them, crying piteously for aid—a fearful scene that made Roger close his eyes to keep from fainting. "If only we could do something for them!" he murmured, but this was not to be.

"They are coming on again, men!" was the cry. "To your posts, and keep your wits about you. Don't dare to fire at more than a hundred yards, and you had better make it eighty. They can't take this place if all of you do your duty."

And then came a second charge in all of its wild and never-to-be-forgotten fury.

CHAPTER XVIII

THE STORMING OF THE REDOUBT

THE slaughter upon the British side had been so terrible that, on retreating, some of the redcoats had gone to their boats with the intention of returning to Boston. But Howe, still calm and still confident of ultimate success, stopped such a proceeding, and presently the arrival of a few reinforcements calmed the spirits of those who had faced the Americans' line of fire, and knew its deadly effects.

"We must take the hill—be the cost what it may!" was the rallying cry, but though the grenadiers and light infantry prepared to advance a second time, their hearts were not so much in the work as they had been earlier in the day. They were beginning to respect those raw peasants at whom they had previously scoffed.

The fire in Charlestown was now at its height, and the wind carried the smoke and burning embers in all directions. From the war vessels and the floating batteries, as well as from the cannon on Copp's Hill, and from the pieces with the British army, came a most terrific bombardment, making a scene that was awful beyond description. And from a distance thousands of spectators viewed the scene—colonists hoping almost against hope that their boys and men would come out victorious, and Tories, British reserves, and English wives of redcoats anxious, but still unwilling to believe but that this day would bring a crushing defeat to all of those who dared oppose the regal will of George III.

Amid the smoke and the screaming of shot and shell, the British troops advanced a second time, Howe at their head, filling not only his own position, but doing the duty of half a dozen fellow officers, who had been cut down in that first assault. "Steady, men, steady!" he called out. "Remember what you are—remember what our noble king expects of you. This is the day when heroes are to be made!" And with a loud rallying cry, grenadiers and infantry pushed on, over the fences, through the tall grass, in some places trampled down into a slippery paste, leaping over the bodies of their countless slain, and not even pausing to carry to the rear those wounded who were crying so piteously for assistance. "We must take the hill first!" was the cry. "The hill first—other things must wait," and they moved on.

The Americans were highly excited, for the first retreat of the enemy had given them the impression that victory was within their grasp. Some had even leaped over the breastworks to go in pursuit, but had been called back by those in command, who knew how foolhardy such a movement would prove. "Here we are, and here we will stay," said Colonel Prescott.

"Yes, we have a good thing here," said General Warren, who was now serving with a musket. "Let us keep it."

The straight line of scarlet coats was not over eight rods away when the order came to fire. Instantly a strong volley rang out, and as the long flashes of fire died away, that advancing line was seen to stagger and break up, two men out of every four falling headlong.

"Load! Load! as quickly as you can!" came the cry from the captain under whom the minute boys were serving. "Down they go, like grass before the scythe! We'll have 'em on the run again in another minute!"

Bang! Crack! Bang! The British had opened, but as before, the aim was either too high or too low, and the bullets flew up into the air or buried themselves in the dirt of the breastworks or the grass at the rail fence. To be sure, a few of the colonists were hit, but the number was nothing in comparison to those struck down outside.

Roger was loading and firing as never before. He had his coat off, and the perspiration was pouring from him in streams. Everybody, wounded and well, was calling for water, but now none was to be had, excepting it be brought from the Neck, and not a man could be spared to fetch it.

"Talk about Concord and Lexington," gasped Dick. "They weren't a circumstance to this."

"Thar's another officer," put in Hen. "Roger, lend me thet flintlock a minit." The musket was forthcoming, the Vermonter rested the muzzle on the dirt, took careful aim, and pulled trigger—and down went the officer flat upon one of his men, already dead. Right or wrong, the colonists did all they could to pick off those in command on this historic day.

The British were serving up their troops, one company after another, at both the breastworks and at the rail fence. The execution was fearful, yet General Howe would not allow a retreat to be sounded. "Once again! Only once again!" he would cry. "I am with you, come on!" and he would dash to the front. Already twelve of his officers had been laid low, yet this gallant commander seemed to bear a charmed life.

The British artillery had come closer, extra horses being attached to the cannon to drag them through the soft meadows, and now they opened up nearly on a line with the breastworks, doing considerable execution. Roger was just reloading his musket, when there came a loud report, and two men behind him pitched forward lifeless. As he gazed at them, he, too, fell prostrate.

"Roger, Roger, are you wounded?" It was the voice of Hen, who had thrown down his gun and rushed to his young master's assistance. "Where are ye hit?"

"I—I'm all—right," came in a gasp. "The—the cannonball—took the wind out of—me!"

"By gum! Thet's gettin' it putty close, lad!"

"I suppose it is." Roger sat up. "Go on and—fight. I'll be all right in a—few—minutes." And he was as white as a sheet, and his face wore a more sober look than it had for a long while past.

In a moment more the British came on ahead, savagely, for the slaughter nerved them for the encounter. Up and up they came, until it looked as if they must pour over the breastworks and the rail fence by sheer force of number and will power. It was a magnificent onslaught, yet it availed nothing, for again and again the deadly American volleys rang out, until the dead and dying on the slopes beyond the defenses barred the progress of the troops that were trying to advance from the rear.

"Once more!" rang out from Howe. "Only once more, my gallant men!" but alas! Brave as was this man, there were none left to listen to him now, for his troops were retreating, and could not be stopped. Pell mell they ran down the hillside and over the fences, straight for their boats. They had had enough—they would not go back, many told each other.

What a cheering arose from the American lines! "We've whipped 'em! See 'em run! What do you think of Yankee Doodle now?" And then that tune was taken up everywhere, while some of the exhausted men fairly danced jigs of joy. At that moment it certainly looked as if the battle of Bunker Hill had come to an end, with total victory upon the American side.

"Is it really over?" asked Roger, sitting down in a circle that the minute boys and Hen occupied.

"It's over fer them poor critters ez lays out yonder," returned Hen. "I reckon there must be nigh on to five hundred of 'em mowed down."

"We lost some men, too—in that last fire from the redcoats and the artillery," answered Roger. "Look, they are carrying at least fifty back!"

"My powder has given out!" cried Dick, on making an examination of his horn. "I thought I had enough left for three cartridges!"

"I have but three cartridges left," announced Roger. A general examination showed that every man and boy was running short of ammunition. At once Colonel Prescott was appealed to.

"You mustn't waste a kernel, men," was Prescott's answer. "I will give you all I have." All that could be scraped up were a few artillery cartridges and these were opened and the powder dealt around as though it were more precious than gold.

A long wait ensued—so long that the Americans half suspected that the British really intended to depart and leave their dead and dying behind. But such was not the case.

"We must take yonder hill," insisted General Howe. "British honor is at stake. If the Americans fortify that hill Boston will be at their mercy. You cannot sail away, for our boats are out in the harbor. Fight, conquer, or die!"

Generals Pigot and Clinton spoke in the same strain. Others, however, demurred. "It is simple butchery!" they said. "The hill cannot be taken, unless the price be far above what it is worth!" Those last words are well worth remembering, when we learn General Greene's reply to them.

At last the disordered troops were placed into columns for that third and final charge. New tactics were now assumed. The soldiers were told to discard their heavy outfits, that they might advance upon them double-quick. They were likewise told not to fire until the very defenses themselves were gained, and that they must rely upon their bayonets. The artillery was also told to advance at any cost, until it could rake the breastworks from side to side.

These orders were obeyed to the letter, and as the artillery poured its hot fire along the breastworks, Roger,

Dick, and the others felt fully the peril of their positions.

"We can't hold—" began Roger, when there came another roar, and in a twinkle he saw Andy Cresson go down, with several men. Poor Andy was shot through the neck, and must have expired instantly. Ben Small was wounded, the cannonball striking a rock which went to pieces, hurling the fragments in all directions, one of which hit Ben on the cheek, leaving a bloody opening.

In a few minutes it was plain to see that the breastworks could no longer be held, and a rush was made for the sally port of the redoubt. The sun had made the ground as dry as tinder, and the dust arose in clouds, nearly choking the colonists. With a ringing cheer the British mounted the breastworks and came after the minutemen, firing as they ran. Then came a volley in return, and scores went down on the threshold of victory.

"Thet's my last shot!" exclaimed Hen. "Oh, fer a dozen more cartridges!"

"I'm empty-handed, too," came from Roger. "If only some reinforcements would come up with more powder!" The reinforcements were on the way, but General Ward had not been urgent enough, and some arrived only to find themselves too late.

Yet the fight was not yet at an end. The breastworks were lost, but the Americans still held the redoubt and a portion of the rail fence. Straight to the redoubt marched the British, and again came a volley from the colonists, who were now discharging their last cartridges. "Club them down!" was the cry, as the glittering bayonets of the redcoats appeared, and now flintlocks were used as clubs, while the few who possessed bayonets and swords used them to every possible advantage.

"The day is ours!" The cry came from Major Pitcairn, he who had ordered that first volley at Lexington, which Roger and the other minute boys remembered so well. Roger heard the cry, and recognized the British officer.

"De day ain't yours, anyway," came softly from a Negro named Salem, and lifting his flintlock quickly, he let fly his last charge—and Pitcairn never lived to view the victory he had helped to make possible.

Officers and men were now falling in every direction. Howe had at last been wounded, in the foot, and was now carried from the field. Colonel Abercrombie of the grenadiers likewise went down, saying almost with his dying breath, of his old friend of days gone by, "If you take Putnam alive, don't hang him, for he's a brave fellow."

The parapet of the redoubt was gained, and over the wall poured the redcoats like a human cataract, the Americans beating them vainly with gun stock, sword, and bayonet. At such short range the fire of the British became as deadly as the fire from our side had formerly been, and to the dust and smoke and general confusion were added the heartrending cries of the fearfully wounded, who, instead of being aided, were, in many cases, trampled under foot.

Colonel Prescott now saw that further fighting was useless. The reinforcements promised had not arrived, his men were out of ammunition and exhausted, and the majority had not even bayonets with which to continue the struggle. Loath as he was to give ground, he felt it his duty to save his forces from complete annihilation, and ordered them to retreat. "We'll fight another day," he said. "Come." And they came, but reluctantly, and growling roundly that no more ammunition was forthcoming.

General Warren did not want to go, and fought to the last. Amid the dust and smoke he waved his weapon on high, as if to bid defiance, single-handed, to the whole British troop. But a volley fired at the retreating colonists rang out, and he fell, mortally wounded. The death of the warmhearted, patriotic doctor, when it became known, produced a profound sensation throughout the colonies, and his taking off was considered little less than a catastrophe.

Almost blinded by the dust and smoke, Roger attempted to retreat with Dick, Hen, and the others. He had been struck in the face by some dirt falling from the crumbling parapet, and now a redcoat leaped

*ROGER WAS HORRIFIED TO SEE HEN PITCH
FORWARD ON HIS FACE*

upon him, as if to run him through with a bayonet. Catching the gun barrel, he thrust the glittering steel aside.

"Not just yet!" he cried, and aimed a blow at the redcoat with his musket stock. The weapon landed as intended, and the youth saw the redcoat roll over and over, and then disappear from view in the confusion which was growing greater every moment.

"Roger!" The cry came from Hen. "This way—ef ye want to save yourself," and the hired man came up on a run and caught the boy by the arm. Scarcely had he done so than a dozen redcoats surrounded the pair. Bayonets flashed to the right and the left and several reports rang out, and Roger was horrified to see Hen pitch forward on his face, the blood flowing from a gaping wound in his neck.

"Hen!" he gasped, and knelt down. He was about to go on, when he felt something pierce his side. He glanced over his shoulder, to behold a bayonet with an ugly looking redcoat behind it; and then of a sudden he felt a pain as of fire, and his senses forsook him.

CHAPTER XIX

Into Boston As a Prisoner

When Roger came to his senses, he found himself lying in the bottom of a barge with the setting sun shining directly in his face. The craft was filled with prisoners and British soldiers, the majority of whom were wounded. He tried to raise himself to a sitting position, but could not, because another lay across his stomach.

"Where—where am I?" he gasped out, but nobody paid any attention to him. Then a number of groans and curses filled his ears, and soon he realized his position—that he was a prisoner of the enemy.

The day had been won by the British but at a fearful cost. They had lost, according to their own estimates, a thousand and forty men, leaving several hundred unaccounted for, and of those who were killed ninety-two were officers. The Americans lost one hundred and fifteen killed and about three hundred wounded.

194

Well might General Greene declare, grimly, that he was "willing to sell 'em another hill at the same price." The British did not want it. They halted on Bunker Hill, while the colonists retreated to the Neck and to Cambridge.

From the start, Colonel Prescott had been the leading figure in this important drama, and now he hastened on horseback to General Ward and begged for more soldiers. "Give me but three regiments—fifteen hundred men—and plenty of ammunition, and I will retake all that has been lost and more," he said. But Ward demurred, for he could not spare the troops, and the stock of ammunition on hand was already dangerously low. He thanked Prescott for what had been accomplished, and let him go. But Prescott had already done enough to win undying fame among those millions who today share in the liberty for which he fought so sturdily.

After leaving the peninsula, the American forces concentrated at Cambridge, Prospect Hill, Winter Hill, Chelsea, and other points of importance, ready to repel any attack the enemy might make. But as before mentioned, the British, "did not want another hill at the same price," and they remained at Bunker Hill and in Boston, much disheartened over their tremendous loss. Out of some companies that had gone out thirty-five and forty strong, only eight to twelve men remained to be commanded by the oldest private, all of the officers having been killed! This was indeed a loss calculated to chill the stoutest heart.

When the sun went down on that Saturday night, all was doubt and uncertainty. The British cannons still roared, sending their shots toward the Neck and other points which the Americans were supposed to be occupying. This firing kept up until three o'clock Sunday afternoon, when a violent rainstorm came up, compelling the gunners to cease because they could not aim their pieces.

Cambridge was crowded with troops coming in from all directions, and with women and children, who came in to learn the fate of fathers, sons, and brothers. Here were also a number of refugees from Charlestown, folks who had either brought their valuables with them or hidden them in dry wells and cellars.

"What will the British do next?" was upon the lips of all, while in Boston a similar question arose in the minds of those who had remained or gone back to the besieged town.

All through that night, so clear overhead, yet so full of gloom, poor Roger lay in the barge, which had been rowed from Moulton's Point to the wharf at the North Battery. He had a bayonet thrust through his right side, but fortunately the flow of blood had ceased, otherwise he must have died where he lay. To his horror, he saw that the man lying partly across him had already breathed his last.

A detachment of three redcoats guarded the barge, and none of them hesitated to crack a prisoner with his musket stock did the poor fellow show any inclination to rise. "Keep where you are," was the command, and Roger wisely concluded to obey.

Barges and other small boats were coming and going, making trips to Moulton's Point and bringing back the British wounded, who were being taken up to the hospital and a dozen other buildings for treatment. From one of the soldiers Roger heard that some twenty Americans had been brought over. "But they must wait," said the redcoat, grimly.

At six o'clock Sunday morning an order came to take the barge from the North Battery Wharf to Long Wharf. At once the boat was shoved off, in charge of a single soldier and a waterman, the latter doing the rowing. The course was directly down the harbor, past what was then termed Clarke's or Hancock's Wharf.

The harbor was filled with shipping, and the waterman had to move slowly, for fear of running into some other craft. "Have a care, man, have a care!" cried the soldier. "I can't swim, and I'm not of a humor to be made food for fishes just yet."

"Water! Water!" murmured one of the wounded colonists. "If you won't give me a drink, throw me overboard and let me drown!" But the redcoat only smiled darkly and shoved him down into his place beside Roger. This act caused Roger's heart to boil with indignation, but he could do nothing either for his fellow prisoner or himself.

The pain had now left the youth, and a strange numbness followed. At times he felt so faint that his senses seemed on the point of forsaking him again. "I wonder if I am badly hurt, and what they will do with me?" were questions that he asked himself many times.

At last Long Wharf was gained and they tied up close to the narrow wooden steps leading down into the water. A dozen other barges were about, and on the wharf stood a score of wagons and carts.

"Where are you hurt?" questioned a kindly looking officer, at the foot of the steps.

"In my side—here—a bayonet stab," murmured the boy. He took half a dozen steps, then staggered, and would have fallen had not the officer braced him up.

"Place him in the second cart," was the order, and two marines lifted Roger between them and carried him to the floor of the wharf. The cart was then ordered up King Street to the deserted residence of one of Boston's leading businessmen—the house having now been turned into a temporary hospital.

The jolting of the cart over the uneven highway caused Roger's wound to bleed afresh, and long before the drive came to an end the minute boy fainted. When he came to his senses he found himself stretched on a mattress laid on the floor, while a British soldier was dressing the wound in his side.

"Coming around, eh?" was the cheery greeting. "Well, you're not so bad off, so the surgeon says. You want to keep quiet for awhile and you'll be all right."

"Can I have drink of water?"

"Certainly—all you will. Here, let me brace your head up with this extra pillow." The soldier did as he desired and soon procured a pitcher of water and a stone mug. "You're rather young to be in such a fight," he observed, while Roger was drinking.

"I am no younger than were lots of others. Thank you for the drink."

"You fought well, I can say that for you."

"Is it all over now?"

"There is no fighting at present, but nobody can tell when it will break out again. Your army has retired beyond Charlestown Neck and we occupy the hill that cost so many lives. Now you had better keep quiet and give your wound a chance to heal," and the soldier turned away to wait on others that were wounded. In his younger days he had served in an apothecary shop, and now he had been pressed into service as a surgeon's assistant. His name was Rufus Montgomery, and Roger saw a good deal of him ere they parted company.

Slowly the hours dragged by. From a distance could be heard the booming of an occasional shot, while from the street came the rattle of the carts and wagons, mingled sometimes with the cries and groans of the wounded and dying. This Sunday in June, 1775, was one that the inhabitants of Boston were not likely to forget so long as they lived, being as it was so full of horror and alarm.

Toward nightfall Rufus Montgomery came again to Roger, this time with a bottle of rum in his hands. "Do you wish some of this to strengthen you?" he questioned.

"I—I don't know," was the youth's reply. "I don't drink, usually, but—but—"

"I will put a few spoonfuls into your water glass and mix it with your drink, as a medicine," said the British soldier, and this was done. The concoction was certainly strengthening, and Roger's pulse, low before, began to pick up.

For supper that evening, the prisoners that were wounded were served with bean soup and stale bread. This may appear a hard fare, but it must be remembered that food in Boston was very scarce, and the soldiers and inhabitants subsisted almost entirely upon beans, pork, and salted fish, with fresh fish when they could be caught. Flour was almost worth its weight in coin, and beef and mutton became an article only to be remembered. But bad as the condition was now, it was to grow infinitely worse as the siege progressed.

Although Montgomery was very considerate of those under his care, he was also strict, and no talking among the prisoners was allowed. There were eight wounded men besides himself in the house, but who they were Roger had no means of ascertaining, excepting by their faces, which proved that they were strangers to him.

"How long will you keep me here?" he asked of Montgomery.

"Until you are well, or at least until you are able to walk around."

"And after that?"

"I cannot answer definitely. Probably you will be put into the jail with the other prisoners."

"Can I send word home that I am alive?"

"Perhaps you'll be able to do that later on. You cannot, however, do it now," was the British attendant's reply, and with this Roger had to be content.

CHAPTER XX

Sad News at Home

The days that followed the battle of Bunker Hill were busy ones in the American army. The lines of defense had to be extended and strengthened, and in the meantime additional troops were called for, and they came in not alone from New England, but from many other places, until it could truly be called our Continental army. And while this was going on, George Washington was called from his retirement and made commander-in-chief.

The coming of Washington produced great changes. Heretofore, the soldiers had been largely without uniforms, and many knew little or nothing concerning actual military tactics and regulations. Leading officers acted largely upon their own responsibilities, and that grand gathering of patriots had been without a supreme head. All was in a raw state and the wisest did not know what was going to happen next, or how political affairs would shape themselves. A few of the most ignorant thought Washington was to be some sort of a war king.

The change came speedily, considering how much had to be accomplished. The defenses which were absolutely necessary to the safety of the army were properly garrisoned, the troops were formed into divisions, and each officer was assigned to his particular duty. A commissary department was organized, so that food so liberally contributed should not go to waste. An urgent appeal for ammunition was made, and Washington saw to it that the military stores were forthcoming. Drunkenness, which had been spreading among those who had now cut away from home influence for the first time, was checked and so severely punished that it almost entirely ceased. By a special order the commander-in-chief had church services held regularly on the Sabbath day, and everybody not actually on duty had to attend. Before long the soldiers were placed in proper uniforms, and every officer from a corporal to a general had instilled into him a proper pride in his position through wearing the insignia of his rank.

Nor was this all that was accomplished. The British were hemmed in by land, but so far, the harbor and the ocean beyond had been free to them. More than once their vessels had gone to prey along the coast and bring back to town the stores which had been confiscated. The Americans soon began to fit out vessels of their own, and presently the British captains found that they must move with caution or run the risk of a battle at sea; and small craft were compelled to remain within the harbor.

The news of the battle of Bunker Hill had reached Mrs. Morse and Dorothy late Saturday night, and Mother and daughter sat up for hours awaiting the tidings from Roger that did not come.

"You had better go to bed, Mother," said the girl, when the tall hallway clock sounded out the hour of three. "It is not likely that anybody will come between now and sunrise."

"Then you go, Dorothy," answered Mrs. Morse. "I cannot sleep."

But Dorothy would not retire, and in the end Mrs. Morse rested herself upon a couch in the sitting room. Morning dawned and the breakfast hour went by, but still nobody came to give them news excepting an old man who had matters far from straight.

"We're whipt!" said this person. "They have kilt all of our brave minutemen! They say Bunker Hill is piled two deep with dead an' dying, an' the blood is turning the Mystic River red!"

"Heaven spare us!" gasped Mrs. Morse. "And my boy, my Roger—" she could not finish.

"I know naught o' Roger," answered the old man.

"But it's a sad day for the colonies an' a great one fer George III, burn him!" and the old man stamped away.

This report caused the two more anxiety than ever, and when church time came Dorothy did not go out, as had always been her habit, but remained at home to administer medicines to her parent, who was growing weaker every hour. It was while she was at this task that she noted a wagon coming slowly along the road from Charlestown Neck.

"Here comes Mr. Cresson, Mother!" she cried. "Surely he must bring news of some sort."

"Yes, yes—run out to the gate and stop him!" returned the parent feebly, and Dorothy ran out to find Mr. Cresson already turning in toward the wide horse block.

"Mr. Cresson, you have news for us?" said the girl, as the farm wagon came to a halt. Then she glanced into the open wagon and saw two bodies covered with a blanket. "Oh!"

"Yes, I have news," was the low answer, and tears filled the minuteman's eyes. "I—I've got two of 'em here—my Andy and Hen Peabody."

"Dead!" And now every bit of color forsook Dorothy's cheeks.

"My Andy is—is dead,"—the man could scarcely utter the words—"Hen is pretty badly wounded. He begged to be brought along, so I fetched him."

"Poor Hen! And Roger?" Dorothy's heart almost

stopped beating as she put the question.

"I know nothing about him—nor could I find out, Dorothy." Mr. Cresson heaved a heavy sigh. "Better fix up a bed for Hen and I'll carry him in."

"I will. But, oh, Mr. Cresson, I am so sorry for you— Andy was such a good boy—he and Roger were such friends!" Dorothy's eyes were swimming in tears and she caught the farmer's browned and wrinkled hand.

"He was—he was—the best of lads, my Andy!" The farmer broke down and sobbed aloud. "My poor, poor boy—how could they kill you?" He drew his hands across his eyes. "I don't know how I'm to tell his mother."

"I would tell her for you, but Mother is worse and Hen must be attended to. Poor Hen! Is he bad?"

"Yes; but he's bandaged up. I had the surgeon do that before I started. Fix the bed, and I'll be on my way."

Into the house and upstairs flew Dorothy, and had the couch ready in a few minutes. Then Mr. Cresson came in, carrying Hen in his arms as if the tall Vermonter were a child. The burden was deposited on the bed, and without waiting to see Mrs. Morse, the farmer left, and drove away slowly, and with downcast head.

"Dorothy!" The word issued from Hen's lips in a whisper, and a half smile played around the hired man's mouth for an instant. "Am I hum?"

"You are, Hen."

"Thank God fer it!" was the heavy answer. "It was a—a fearful fight. I never want tew see anuther like it."

"You are badly wounded, Hen."

"Wall, I reckon it ain't no flea bite, Miss Dorothy. I—I—will ye give me a drink o' water?"

"Yes, yes!" The girl fairly flew for the water crock in the kitchen. When she returned, the Vermonter had fainted.

It was not until Monday morning that Hen opened his eyes again. In the meantime a doctor had been stopped, as he was passing by on his way to Cambridge, and he had prescribed for the unfortunate sufferer. "Dress his wound daily and keep him quiet," were the orders. "Give him broth and such things, and a little liquor when he looks to be sinking, but do not give him too much, as he may go into a fever."

The beginning of the week brought new horrors, as it was learned that this one or that was either dead or wounded. One house out of every three was in mourning for some father, brother, or near relative. It was now that the hearts of those who looked for freedom were tried as with fire. Should they turn back and submit to the king, or should the struggle continue?

"If only I could learn something of Roger!" sighed Dorothy, and her mother nodded mutely. Roger was in their minds constantly, but as yet no word had come to them of him.

On Wednesday Nellie Winthrop presented herself at the door, carrying a traveling bag in her hand.

"I have come over to help you," she explained. "I know Hen must be a great care, and I thought you would like me to come."

"It is very kind of you," said Dorothy, warmly. "If they can spare you at home, you'll be more than welcome here."

Mrs. Morse was worse, and Dorothy utterly worn out. Nellie knew well how to take hold, and soon made Roger's sister retire. When Mrs. Morse and Dorothy were both asleep, she turned her attention to Hen, who had lain in a stupor for twenty-four hours, just rousing sufficiently now and then to call for a drink.

She had found the Vermonter's brow as hot as fire, and catching hold of his wrist, felt his pulse beating rapidly.

"He is going to have the fever, after all," she thought. "Poor fellow, I wonder if he doesn't know something about Roger?" And then she busied herself to make sure that the bandage on Hen's neck had not shifted. Besides the wound on his neck, the hired man also suffered from a sword thrust through his thigh.

Toward sundown Nellie found the house very quiet, and she walked out into the dooryard, to get a bit of fresh air. She could not get Roger out of her mind, for as we know, these two young people thought a good deal of each other.

"Nellie Winthrop, is that you?"

The call came from the roadway, and looking up she saw Mr. Small standing there, his arm in a sling, for he had been wounded, too. At once she ran to the farmer.

"Yes, I am here, helping Dorothy care for her mother and for Hen Peabody, who has been wounded," she explained. "And you are hurt, too. Too bad!"

"It is not much." Mr. Small looked at her seriously. "I've got bad news for the folks here," he went on.

"Bad news? Of Roger?"

"Yes; the poor boy was shot down in the fight."

"And is he dead?" Nellie had to force herself to speak the words.

"I can't tell you absolutely, but I reckon he is, and the captain of the company thinks the same. You see, the fight got so hot he had to be left behind. But I saw him stabbed with a bayonet and go down, and—My gracious, Nellie, what's the matter? If you— The gal's fainted!"

Randolph Small was right, the shock had proved too much, and now Nellie lay like one dead in his uninjured arm. Tenderly he carried her into the house, and the noise of caring for her aroused Dorothy.

"Something must have happened, Mr. Small," said

Roger's sister, taking in the situation by instinct rather than by reason. "You—you have brought bad news?"

"Let us help the gal first, Miss Dorothy."

"But Roger—Oh, if you know anything, tell me all. Anything is better than this suspense."

Dorothy clasped her hands and looked into his face so imploringly that he could not resist, and blurted out all—how the tide of battle had swept him close to Roger, how the redcoats had advanced on the boy and on Hen, and how he had seen both go down before that glistening bunch of bayonets. "Hen was carried off by the crowd through the dust and smoke," he concluded, "but Roger went down, and the last I saw of him the British were tramping over him."

"Then Roger is dead!" The cry came from the doorway, and Mrs. Morse stood before them. "Oh, my boy, my poor, dear boy!" And turning, she staggered to her couch, not to rise from it for many a weary month to come.

There was but one thing that kept Dorothy up, the knowledge that her duty to her mother, to Nellie, and to the faithful hired man must be done, regardless of what had happened to sadden her youthful heart. Drying her tears as fast as they followed, she set about reviving her parent and her friend, and by the time this was accomplished, the first shock was past, and she felt better. Soon she saw her mother slip on her knees in prayer. She joined at her side, and as her parent uttered the words, "Oh, Father in heaven, thy will, not ours, be done," she murmured "Amen." Then the load was lifted, even though the spot where it had rested was still sore.

CHAPTER XXI

URIAH BEDWELL'S THREAT

"WELL, Morse, you are to be removed today."

It was Rufus Montgomery who spoke, and he addressed Roger, who sat in a stiff backed chair, gazing out of the window of the mansion which had, under British rule, become a temporary hospital.

The first of September had come and gone, and Roger felt a good bit like his old self, although his side was still stiff, and he felt 'compelled to move about with care. He had been allowed to exercise himself daily now for two weeks, under the watchful eye of a corporal of marines. The distance covered each day was to Long Wharf and back, or to the Town Dock, through Crooked Lane. Once his guard had taken him to the neighborhood of the Old South Meetinghouse, which was now being used as a riding academy.

"And where am I to go, Montgomery?" asked Roger.

"Do you deem it necessary to ask, Morse? Where

would you expect to go from here?" And the surgeon's assistant, who had taken a fancy to the youth because of his open and manly way, smiled sadly.

"I presume I am to be removed to a jail."

"Exactly. You have been pronounced by Doctor Wells to be sufficiently recovered to join the other prisoners."

"Will they take me to the prison at the Court House?"

"I hardly think so, for that place is greatly overcrowded. There is another stone building several blocks south of here. More than likely they will place you there. We Englishmen call it the Owl's Rest."

"I've heard of that resort," said Roger, with a little shiver. "It was formerly some sort of an iron foundry, and has very small windows and a tall chimney."

"That is the spot—scarcely as attractive as this. To tell the truth, I am very sorry for you, Morse; you'd be quite the proper sort if you weren't a rebel."

"Thank you, Montgomery, and you're the right sort, too," answered Roger. "I'll not forget you nor the splendid treatment I have received at your hands. If I ever have a chance to return your goodness I'll try to do it, and with interest," and then the pair shook hands.

Half an hour later a prison guard of eight grenadiers marched up, and the sergeant in command presented an order for Roger and three others. Soon the little party was on the way, along a street that was fairly baked with the midsummer sun. Hardly a soul was in sight, and here and there the grass was growing high between the pavements. Truly, Boston was not a town to be envied in those tiresome days of the siege.

The walk again took Roger past the Old South Meetinghouse, located on the corner of what was then Milk and Marlborough streets. Here the pews had been taken out, some of the doors shut up, and many loads of dirt carted in, that the redcoats might have a sheltered place in which to ride. Around the church were many fine trees, but several of these had been hacked down for firewood. The well-known Liberty Tree, standing at what is now the corner of Essex and Washington Streets, was also cut down for fuel, and when it fell one of the soldiers aiding in its destruction was killed.

"There is Gage's residence," whispered one of the prisoners to Roger, and nodded to a fine looking brick mansion opposite to the church. This was the Province House, a three-storied structure, topped by a cupola, upon which was perched the figure of an Indian with drawn bow and arrow.

The prisoner had scarcely spoken when there rolled from the grounds in front of the house an elegant chariot, drawn by a team of fiery horses. Instantly the sergeant halted his grenadiers, and all presented arms in the stiffest of military uniforms. They were

Generals Gage and Burgoyne.

The party continued on its way down Malborough Street to Summer, passing Trinity Church, at that time a plain building of wood, ninety feet deep by sixty feet broad, and boasting of nothing better than a simple sloping roof, without cupola or steeple. Then they came to a big, wet pasture known as Rowe's field, but long since filled in and covered with hundreds of handsome stores and dwellings.

The dingy building Roger had heard of loomed up before them and an oaken door opened to receive them. Within all was dark and dirty, with a foul odor that was sickening. "Must I really stay in this hole?" thought the youth, and hesitated on the threshold. But a slap from the flat side of a sword made him realize his position, and he passed on.

Originally the foundry had been an open place, not unlike a large blacksmith shop, but now the British had divided its single floor into several apartments, one being given over to the guard and the others to the prisoners. Behind the building were a whipping post and a pillory, to be used when prisoners broke the prison regulations.

"This is simply awful!" thought Roger, as he surveyed the apartment into which he had been led. Overhead the ceiling was thick with smoke, dirt, and cobwebs, and the walls were no better, while the flooring was covered with broken up and foul smelling straw. One window, two feet square and heavily barred, gave what there was of light and ventilation.

"This is beastly!" muttered a fellow prisoner. "Morse, we'll soon die here."

"I shouldn't wonder, Conroy." Roger gave a groan. "I suppose we are to sleep on this," and he kicked up some of the short straw, dismally.

"Yes, sleep on it, sit on it, and dine on it, for all I know to the contrary," growled Conroy, who was a militiaman from Connecticut. "Oh, but I hope Old Put captures this town soon!" Like many other men from his state, Conroy believed that there was no greater military man than dashing Israel Putnam.

The march had been a quick one, and Roger was quite exhausted. Looking around, he found a fairly clean corner and threw himself down, giving himself up to reflections which were far from pleasant. Conroy continued to pace the floor moodily.

To go into the details of what happened during that never-to-be-forgotten winter would be superfluous. Each day was like those which had gone before, only more wearisome and discouraging. The only bright spots were the half hour allowed each day for an airing, when the prisoners marched out by twos, chained together, for a tour of the meadow.

At the end of the time mentioned, Roger was himself

THE WALK AGAIN TOOK ROGER PAST THE OLD SOUTH MEETINGHOUSE

again, so far as his wound went. Otherwise, however, he was growing thinner daily, and his hollow cheeks and the deep rings under his eyes told only too plainly how the boy suffered.

Food was scarcer than ever, and the daily fare was pork and beans, with dried or salted fish on Sundays. Of fresh meat there was not an ounce, even the guard declaring that he had forgotten how a roast or a steak tasted. For drinking they had water, and tea, if they wanted it, but the minutemen refused the latter against principle, having sworn to drink none of the beverage until America was free. Rum could also be had in plenty, if a prisoner was willing to pay the price that was asked, sixpence a glass. Liquor, being cheap in the town at large, caused much drunkenness among the British soldiers, until General Gage made the penalty for intoxication very severe.

One day in early September, Roger was out for his airing, chained to Conroy, when, on moving along the highway which skirted the meadow, he came face to face with Uriah Bedwell and Deacon Marston. For the moment none of the three could believe that they had seen right.

"You!" burst from Uriah Bedwell.

"It's that Morse boy!" exclaimed Deacon Marston. "A prisoner!"

"Yes, I am a prisoner," answered Roger, bitterly.

"What of it?"

"Well, it—er—it serves you right," answered Bedwell, sourly. "I hope they hang you!"

"Thank you, Mr. Bedwell, that is no more than I would expect from such an unscrupulous Tory as you."

"Ha! This to me—and in Boston!" gasped the lawyer, in a rage. "Guard, did you hear what he said?"

"I did, sir," answered the corporal in charge.

"He insulted me!"

"And you said you hoped they would hang me," put in Roger.

"They ought to hang you!"

"What is the boy guilty of, sir?" asked the corporal, with interest.

"A good deal. Through his instrumentality was I driven from my home, and my house was burnt to the ground," fumed Bedwell.

"And he brought several false charges against me," added Barnaby Marston. "He is a thorough villain!"

"In that case you had better report him to General Howe, sirs."

Uriah Bedwell frowned darkly. "I will see about that. You have him a prisoner below here?" and he waved his hand in the direction.

"We have."

"Take good care that he does not escape. He is a slick young rascal."

"No slicker than you are," cried Roger. "Even if I am a prisoner, Uriah Bedwell, I am not afraid of you nor of the charges you may bring against me. Even if he is our enemy, General Howe is a gentleman, and I am certain he will listen to my story as well as to yours. You had a perfect right to turn Tory if your heart told you to do so, but you had no right, legal or moral, to secretly plot to ruin the neighbors who had made you what you are."

"Tut, tut, boy, don't say another word!" The Tory shook his fist, vigorously. "Just wait, and you'll learn a thing or two!" and he stalked off in high dudgeon, with Marston following.

This meeting caused Roger to do a deal of thinking, and for two days he watched for Bedwell's appearance at the prison, but the Tory failed to put in an appearance.

"Reckon he's afraid of what you may have to tell about him," observed Conroy, to whom Roger had long since told his story. "Some of those Tories are the meanest men on earth. I'd jest as lief put up with a British backslider as with any of 'em."

That night Conroy got into difficulty with the jailer who brought him his food. Some sharp words followed, and the prisoner, who lay on the damp straw, received a heavy kick in his side.

"Oh!" he groaned. Then he raised up and with a face full of bitter hatred glared at the jailer. "I'll remember you for that! One of these days you'll be sorry you did it!" Roger heard the words, but paid no special attention at the time, but it was not many days ere he had good cause to remember them.

All told, there were twenty-two prisoners in the old foundry, including six that occupied the apartment in which the boy had been placed. But the day after the assault just mentioned, twelve of the prisoners were taken away to the Court House building, and among them were those who had shared quarters with Roger and the Connecticut man. At the same time, the guard was reduced from twelve to six soldiers, with one Negro cook to prepare the scanty food provided.

"I see our clown ain't gone," grumbled Conroy, referring to the jailer with whom he had had trouble. "Worst luck."

The British soldier overheard this remark, and in consequence Conroy was subjected that afternoon to ten lashes on his bare back at the whipping post behind the jail, and he was, moreover, deprived of both eating and drinking for the balance of the day.

"This is a shame," said Roger to him, when he got the chance. "Conroy, you can have half of my supper and welcome."

"Don't want it—it would choke me," was the answer, in suppressed rage. "Oh, what a villain Corporal Grumbert is! If only I had a sword, how I would love to run him through and through! But my time will come!" And the man threw himself in a heap in a corner and refused to be comforted.

During the following afternoon, both Roger and Conroy overheard the guards talking about an inspection of the troops to take place on Boston Common that afternoon. All of the redcoats but Corporal Grumbert and one private were to take themselves away, and were not to show up at the prison again until the following morning. Conroy drank in every word of the talk, and his eyes glistened hatefully. "Now is my chance!" he muttered to himself. "And if they hang me for it, what will it matter?"

CHAPTER XXII

The Vault in the Old Burying Ground

Roger noticed that his companion was very restless during the evening, but as this was nothing unusual, paid no attention. At nine o'clock, for the want of something better to do, the boy threw himself down and fell into a sound sleep.

He awoke with a start, to find Conroy clutching him by the arm. The Connecticut man held one hand over the lad's mouth.

"Hush!" he whispered. "Get up and follow me—if you want to escape!"

"Escape!" spluttered Roger. He was almost stunned by the intelligence.

"Yes, but make no noise, or the guard at the other end of the prison will hear you."

"But how can we escape?" questioned the youth, in a low tone.

"Follow me, and I will show you. Hurry, or it

will be too late."

Without further queries Roger sprang up and came after Conroy, who had advanced to the square window, the sill of which was on a level with their heads. In the dim light of the night, Roger saw that two of the window bars had been removed, leaving a space just wide enough for a man's body.

"Push yourself through, catch hold of the bars and then drop," whispered Conroy. "I'll go first."

"But the guard?"

"Cabot is at the other end of the jail, and as he is singing, I reckon he is pretty well filled with rum."

"And Corporal Grumbert?"

"He won't bother us," was the grim answer. "But hurry, or our chance will be gone. No more pork and beans and whipping post for me!" And so speaking, the Connecticut man raised himself up to the window, pushed himself through, and disappeared from view.

With his heart beating violently, Roger followed, to drop outside upon a patch of wet grass. Already Conroy was skulking along a ditch dug to drain the water away from the old foundry. Roger paused for an instant and caught a line of the drinking song Cabot was humming. "I wonder where Grumbert is?" he asked himself, but never once guessed the horrible truth.

A few stars were shining, but there was no moon, and as silently as ghosts the two stole along the ditch until the road leading into Marlborough Street was gained. Once or twice Roger started to speak, but each time Conroy checked him. "Be silent—we carry our lives in our hands," whispered the minuteman from Connecticut.

"But where are we to go?"

"I thought we might make our way through Frog Lane to the burying ground and then over to the water near Fox Hill. From there, if we can obtain a small boat, we can easily row to the Charles River, where we will be safe."

After this nothing more was said for fully ten minutes, during which time they emerged upon Marlborough Street and hurried southward to Newbury Street, both now known as Washington Street, and then westward into Frog Lane, since christened Boylston Street. At this date Frog Lane was nothing but a country road, deep with mire, and upon either side were frog ponds of generous area, whence the name. On the upper side was the burying ground and at the foot was a swamp ground, now filled in to the distance of a dozen city blocks, and covered with handsome stores and dwellings.

"Stop!" The command came from Conroy, as he clutched Roger by the arm. From out of the gloom the pair had seen a dozen redcoats advancing, their tower muskets on their shoulders. Evidently they were some relief guards on picket duty along the shore to the south of Fox Hill.

They stopped and sought shelter behind a number of trees in the burying ground. Roger held his breath. Had they been seen? Fervently he prayed not.

"Who goes there?" The cry came from the officer in charge of the guard.

Of course no answer was returned. Instantly the officer brought his little command to a halt.

"I could have sworn I saw somebody," he muttered. "Men, did you see someone?"

"I saw two persons, over yonder," answered a tall grenadier in the front rank.

"And where did they go to?"

"Toward the burying ground."

"Ha! We must investigate this. Forward!" and the guard came close to where Roger and Conroy were in hiding. "Scatter, men, and see if you can't rout them out," was the next command.

Instantly the soldiers, eight in number, did as commanded, running hither and thither among the trees and over the graves. Soon several of them passed within three yards of the pair in hiding. Roger's heart beat so violently he felt certain the enemies must hear it.

"We must get out of here," whispered Conroy into his ear. "I don't intend to be taken alive," and off he glided like a snake through the grass.

Not wishing to be left alone, Roger started to follow

him, but now came a cracking of dry branches, and
two grenadiers came to a halt directly in front of where
he lay, between a raised vault and a clump of bushes.
As there was no help for it, he remained where he
was, crouching closer to the brush than ever.

"I saw someone here, Darby," said one grenadier.

"So did I," was the reply, "but where did the fellow
go to?"

"I'll give that up."

"Let us search the vicinity."

"Very well, you go around the vault that way and
I'll go this way."

At once the grenadiers moved as agreed, the course
of both taking them around to the bushes behind which
Roger was in hiding.

The boy gave himself up as lost and fell back against
the vault. If he was caught now, what would they do
with him?

"If I could only get up a tree, or something," he
mused. Then he thought of the vault door, almost behind
him. He felt of the barrier and pushed upon it. There
was a faint creaking of the rusty iron hinges, and the
door gave way. Without thinking twice, Roger crept
into the vault and closed the door behind him.

A damp, unwholesome odor greeted him and caused
him to shiver. What a place in which to seek safety!
But anything was better than to be captured, and with

his hands before him he moved to the back end of the sepulchre, between stone biers upon which rested several hermetically sealed coffins.

"I wonder if Conroy is safe?" he mused, when, coming to the rear wall of the vault, he sank down in a corner. His feet had touched several loose boards, and these he now stood up in front of him.

Presently came the creaking of the door again, and he heard the voice of the officer in charge of the guard. "It will do no harm to look inside," the Englishman was saying. The flare of a torch lit up the interior of the sepulchre.

"I'm a goner now!" murmured Roger, as a grenadier pushed his way between coffins. "I might as well give myself up and have done with it."

But though he thought thus, he remained quiet. Soon the grenadier stood directly in front of the slanting boards. Then a shot rang out, coming from the upper end of the graveyard. The shot was followed by a second and a third.

"They've discovered something," cried the British officer. "Come, men, or we will be too late!" and he dashed from the vault. The two grenadiers went after him, banging the door shut as they left, and Roger was alone once more.

For fully ten minutes the youth did not dare to stir. With strained ears he tried to catch what was going on outside, but on the exterior the vault was banked up with sods and no sound penetrated to the interior.

"They must have caught Conroy, or wounded him," he thought, dismally, but he was mistaken. Though seen and fired upon, the Connecticut man had, for the time being at least made his escape.

What should be his next movement? Long and earnestly Roger revolved this problem in his mind without coming to any definite conclusion. He was free it was true, but it would hardly do to show his face in Boston, even among such Whigs as might be willing to befriend him. British orders were becoming stricter every day, and those known to be in sympathy with the colonists scarcely dared to call their souls their own. Walking on the streets of the town after dark was prohibited excepting one had a pass, and no citizen dared to stop another for a friendly chat, unless a guard was present to listen to what was said. As the siege advanced the British became more and more suspicious that the "rebels" in the town were secretly plotting to deliver them into the hands of their enemies, whose fortifications at Prospect Hill, Winter Hill, and elsewhere were growing more formidable every day.

The night was well advanced—in another hour dawn would begin to show itself. If Roger was to act at all he must do so quickly. To remain in this awful place until the next night, without food or drink, was out of the question.

"I must reach the water somehow," he said to himself. "If I throw off my coat and shoes, I can easily swim across the Charles River, if I keep where the water is shallow, so I can wade part of the distance. Anything will be better than this," and he gave a shudder as he moved to the door of the vault.

All was pitch dark, and finding the door was not easy. But after bumping into several coffins, the iron barrier was gained, and he pushed upon it, easily at first, then harder and harder. It refused to budge, and in frantic haste he felt for a knob or a latch. None could be found, for the latch was only upon the outside. Then the horrifying truth burst upon him. He was a prisoner within the vault of the dead.

CHAPTER XXIII

At the Sign of the Shaving Mug

"Locked in!"

The words came from Roger with a groan, and the heavy beads of perspiration stood out upon his forehead. The realization of the true condition of affairs came to him as a shock.

In vain he tried to force the door. It could not be moved the fraction of an inch, and at the end of five minutes, panting for breath, he gave up the effort. So overcome was he by his emotions that he fairly staggered against one of the coffins for support.

"Locked in!" he repeated. "Now what am I to do? Supposing nobody comes to let me out? I will die of hunger and thirst!" He bit his lips until the blood came, and kept back the tears with difficulty. "Oh, this is ten times worse than if I had remained in the prison!"

For half an hour he remained by the door, trying to conjure up some way of opening the barrier between himself and freedom. Nothing could be done, although he tried half a dozen things. Then he walked around among the coffins and along the walls, feeling for some other opening.

Presently his hand struck a niche, and his fingers closed over a candle and a flint and tinderbox. "Thank heaven for the light!" he murmured, and lost no time in striking the flint. But the tinder was damp, and he had to strike and blow diligently for some minutes before he managed to secure a flame. Candle, flint, and box had evidently been left there by somebody who was in the habit of visiting the vault occasionally.

"If only they would come tomorrow!" thought poor Roger. "I would not mind if it was General Howe himself, providing he let me out!"

Candle in hand, the youth made a closer inspection of the door, and then moved along the walls. As he passed one coffin after another he could not help but notice the plates.

Suddenly he started, and the candle almost fell from his hand. "Can this be possible?" he gasped.

The silver plate on a coffin directly before him had riveted his attention. The plate read as follows:

Alan Godfrey Brascoe.
Born in London, Sept. ye 21, 1736.
Killed at ye Battle of Lexington, in Massachusetts,
Apr. ye 19, 1775.

"It must be the same—his wife must have had his body placed here—perhaps until she has a chance to send it back to England," mused Roger, and his mind went back to that fateful day when he had been called to Lieutenant Brascoe's side by the stone wall. Well did he remember the dying man's words and his own promise to return that precious packet of papers to his widow. But the papers were still locked up in that old-fashioned secretary at home, and of Brascoe's widow he had as yet heard nothing.

The coffin was sealed up, but even if this had not been so, it is doubtful if Roger would have cared to look within, so unstrung did he feel over his unusual position. His one thought was of liberty, and soon the Brascoe incident was forgotten.

At the rear of the vault, he came upon a small well like opening. This connected with a trench, running under the vault's back wall. It was placed there for drainage purposes, and was choked up with dry leaves and muck.

Setting down the candle and taking up a bit of board, Roger used the latter as a spade, and began to clean out the drainway. Soon it grew larger, and on looking down he was overjoyed to see daylight streaming through. He continued his labors, and in an hour had a fair sized opening made, leading to one of the cemetery draining ditches.

Blowing out the candle, he crawled through the drainway, and soon found himself breathing the pure air beyond again. My young readers can well imagine what a sigh of relief escaped him when he found himself free. "No more vaults for me," he murmured. "I'll go to prison a dozen times over first!"

The sun was coming up, and he felt that he must move with extreme caution. To get out of Boston during the daylight he felt was impossible. He must find a new hiding place and something to eat and drink, and then await the coming of another night.

As has been mentioned, the Common was directly to the north of the graveyard. Within sight of the burial plot were located several regiments of marines, their lines of tents stretching along the Mall, then called Common Street. Only the tall fence separated Roger from his enemies at this point.

As Roger paused close to one corner of the grounds behind a bush he saw a big farm wagon come along, drawn by a sturdy team of oxen. The wagon was filled with grain, and on the seat sat an elderly man clad in a smock frock.

"Hi, hi, boy! What are you doing here?" came a sudden cry, and looking back, Roger saw a marine advancing toward him. The marine had a musket in his hand, although he was not on guard.

"I'm not hurting anything," returned Roger, as

coolly as he could.

"Where did you come from?"

"I came from the Long Wharf," was the boy's rejoinder, which was strictly true, although a good many months had elapsed since that time.

"Long Wharf, eh? Down here for grain?"

"I was just looking around. Got any grain to spare?"

"No grain for anybody but the faithful. I'll wager you're a Whig."

"I'm more of a hungry boy just now."

At this sally the marine laughed. "Are you, indeed? Well, I can't help you out, for I'm on short rations myself. Get along, or I'll have to put you in the lockup. No loiterers are allowed around here."

"Will they allow me to try fishing over on the flats?" and Roger waved his hand westward.

"No, lad, only soldiers are allowed over there. Get along now—the officer of the guard is coming." And Roger did get along, glad to think he had escaped arrest so easily. Evidently the soldier had not yet received a description of Conroy and himself.

The wagon with grain had gone past, and, struck with a sudden idea, Roger ran toward it and hopped on behind. Perhaps in the heart of the city he would be safer than on the outskirts.

"If I can only find some friend who will house me until this excitement blows over," he thought. "Anyway,

I must get something to eat and to drink, and I haven't
so much as a half penny with me."

The farmer driving the ox team was somewhat deaf,
so he did not hear Roger climb among his bags of grain.
Soon the boy was out of sight. And now for once luck
was with him. Mixed with the grain was a sack of fall
pippins, and digging a hole in the bag Roger pulled
forth half a dozen of the apples and placed them in
his pockets, and then began to devour an apple with
all the gusto that only extreme hunger knows.

Up into the busiest part of Boston rumbled the
heavy wagon, through School Street and past King's
Chapel, which had been chosen by the British as their
public place of worship during their occupation of
Boston. Then the wagon turned into a small side street
and came to a halt before a pothouse, known as the
Shaving Mug, why, nobody could ever say, excepting
that the original proprietor had once been a surgeon
and barber.

The ox team had scarcely come to a standstill, than
a woman came from the Shaving Mug, followed by several
British soldiers.

"Old Oxley is back!" cried one of the soldiers, and
hurried away, followed by the others. The woman ran
to the wagon.

"Why did you not come sooner?" she cried. "They drank
all of the rum and paid not a penny, and now they are gone."

"You should have locked the door upon them," answered the man in the smock frock. "Pity 'tis Peter is dead, or we'd have no such goings on around here."

"Peter is dead, and I wish I was dead, too!" sobbed the woman. "Drive around to the rear, and we'll lock up and count our loss. If I dared—"

"Hush! Your life is not safe if you say what you think, Mollie," returned the old man, and led his ox team up into an alleyway between the pothouse and a two-storied mansion of stone which seemed to be locked up securely from bottom to top.

Roger had listened to the conversation with interest, he hearing easily, as both the deaf man and the woman spoke loudly. Now as the wagon came again to a halt, he leaped down, and seeing a door open to a kitchen, he ran into the apartment.

"Who are you?" cried the woman, as she followed him inside. The man came after the pair, and seeing this, Roger closed the door.

"The British are after me," answered the boy quickly. "I need food, and a place in which to hide until tonight or tomorrow. I do not know you, but you look like kind people, and—"

"Is this some trick?" demanded the woman.

"It is no trick, Madam, I will give you my word of honor."

"And why should we shelter you? Do you not know

that we would be taking a great risk by so doing?"

"I know that, but, but—"

"I know you," broke in the old man. "You are from Lexington, and your name is Morse. Am I not right?"

"You are, sir. But—but—please do not tell anybody."

"Don't ye fear, lad. We understand, eh, Mollie? Are the soldiers close on your heels?"

"Not very. But you see, I broke out of prison, and—"

At that very moment the door of the drinking room in the front of the house opened, and two men entered. At once the woman sprang to Roger's side.

"Into there with you," she said, pointing to a closet. "I will give you all the food you want later on. Now I must attend to my customers."

She shoved him toward the little apartment mentioned. As soon as he was inside, she locked the door, placing the key in the pocket of her apron. Then she hurried to the drinking room, while the old man went out to attend his ox team and his load.

CHAPTER XXIV

THE TORY'S LITTLE PLOT

IT may seem queer that Roger should have applied to the keeper of a drinking place for assistance, when it is remembered that he did not use liquor himself.

But my young readers must recollect that the town of Boston was in a state of siege, and that very few places of any sort were open. Many of the shops had nothing to sell. Fully half of the houses in the town were not only locked but nailed up, with heavy boards placed over the windows. Moreover, the streets, as already mentioned, were almost deserted, and where to go the lad did not know. Chance had placed him in contact with Mollie Stoker and her aged father, Asa Oxley, and he was inclined to make the best of it, understanding only too well that "necessity knows no law."

The closet was broad and deep, more like a dark room than anything else. It contained several suits of clothing, and numerous odds and ends which need not be mentioned here. Against the back wall was a high, iron-bound trunk, which had evidently come from England in one of the Pilgrim's ships. On this trunk Roger sat down, to wait and to speculate upon the new turn of affairs.

The youth had hardly settled himself that he heard voices proceeding from somewhere close to the rear of the closet. Pushing aside some of the clothing, he found that the apartment had been built with two doors, one opening into the kitchen, and the other into the taproom. The latter was nailed up, but a keyhole and a generous crack remained unobstructed. Against the other side of the door rested a table, and at this sat the two men who had just come in to be served.

"Uriah Bedwell and Deacon Marston as sure as fate!" thought Roger. He was right, the couple were indeed the two Tories with whom he had had so much to do in the past.

Both men were drinking leisurely, and talking in low but earnest tones. At first Roger failed to catch much of what was said, but presently his ear became better trained to the situation, and he lost scarcely a word.

"You are a lucky dog, Uriah," he heard Marston observe, as he sat down his glass. "This will mean two thousand pounds in your pocket, if not more."

"Providing you do not fail me, Barnaby," was Bedwell's dry and rather uneasy response.

"Did I ever fail you?"

"Not exactly, but there are times when your backbone is not what it might be."

"I will do what you desire, never fear. But my share—"

"You shall have a fifth, as I promised you before."

"And when will the money come to me?"

"As soon as Alan Brascoe's widow gives up the case, and returns to England."

"She will not go until the British leave Boston."

"That may be true, but—"

"But what?"

"We can well afford to wait. Such a sum of money is not to be sneezed at."

After this came a pause, during which both men called for more liquor, and for a couple of pipes of tobacco. Mollie Stoker waited upon them, and then turned her attention to an English officer who came in to settle a score which had been running for some time.

"Did you not have a deal of trouble with Mrs. Brascoe?" observed Barnaby Marston, after lighting his pipe.

"To be sure. At first she would not believe that her husband was dead."

"But you had plenty of witnesses to that fact."

"Yes, and I—ahem—I sent the body to her, in a coffin I purchased in Cambridge. It lies in the burying ground vault."

"Didn't Brascoe leave any papers regarding the property?"

"She says so, but she also says she cannot find them."

"Perhaps that is merely a blind."

"I think so, and still—" Uriah Bedwell's face clouded. "If she brought to light the right kind of papers, it might prove very awkward for me."

"Did Brascoe's body have the papers on it when it was found?"

"Well—er—ahem, no, nothing, absolutely nothing." Uriah Bedwell heaved a long sigh. "If there are any papers I wish I had them."

Again there was a spell of silence during which Roger scarcely dared to breathe. What he had heard filled him with astonishment, not unmingled with satisfaction. He felt sure that the papers in his possession were *the* papers, and if that was so, he mentally vowed that Alan Brascoe's widow should have them before he attempted to quit Boston.

"Where was Brascoe killed?" asked Marston.

"In Lexington, back of Morse's farm."

"Morse again! That fellow turns up everywhere."

"He is not turning up just now. The guards are

looking for him in vain."

"And what of that other prisoner who escaped?"

"He is gone, too."

"Can it be possible that both escaped to the mainland?"

"I don't know. Those minutemen seem to be able to do wonders when they set out for it. I am afraid before this trouble comes to an end, they will burn the towns over our heads."

"They won't dare do that. Howe will lay the whole country low for twenty miles around," answered Barnaby Marston, and then the two arose, paid their score, and sauntered out. In the meantime, the British officer had left, and now Mollie Stoker barred her front door, that no one else might enter.

"I am sorry to keep you waiting so long, but I have to attend to the customers, or they may pull the house down," she said, half apologetically. "Now no more can enter, and you can come into the kitchen, and I will get you a hot dinner in a few minutes. You look very tired."

"I am tired and hungry, and more hungry than tired," laughed Roger, faintly.

"Won't you have a glass of liquor?"

"Thank you, but I would prefer something to eat."

"But the liquor you must have, lad. I will run and get you a glass of my best," and before Mollie Stoker could be stopped she had reentered her taproom and poured out a generous glass of high spirits.

Roger scarcely knew what to do. He had been brought up in strict temperance by his mother, and to go back on the word he had given her was out of the question, while at the same time he did not wish to offend one who was trying to befriend him.

"Now drink heartily," said the woman. "It will do you a world of good. My late husband laid that cask down eight years ago."

"I—I—would rather not," stammered the youth. "If you will only give me something to eat it will be all right."

"What, you won't drink the liquor!" came in shrill tones. "Boy, are you one of the temperance kind, answer me?"

"If you must know, yes. But supposing we drop that matter and—"

"But I'll not drop it!" Mollie Stoker brought her fist down on the table with a bang. "Temperance, indeed! I'd just as lief give aid to a Tory or to a redcoat! Out of my house this instant!" And running to the alleyway door she threw it wide open.

Roger was about to remonstrate, but one look into those wrathful eyes caused him to change his mind. "All right, I'll go, if you won't help a fellow creature just because he won't drink," he said, in a low voice.

"But let me tell you that you are not the woman I took you to be," and pulling his hat down over his eyes, he darted forth, and ran down the alley to where it came to an end among half a dozen barns and sheds.

At one barn he saw old Oxley unloading his grain, and moved on without speaking to him. Several hundred feet farther on was another barn, close to the rear of a fine brick mansion. The doors stood wide open and he hurried within, to gain his breath and lay plans for future movements. He felt like a fox that is being run down by the huntsmen.

From the rear of the barn came the voice of a Negro, singing softly to himself as he cleaned off a beautiful black horse.

"He'll be no friend," thought Roger, as he recognized the song as one the British soldiers were wont to sing—one telling of what was to be done with the rebels who were to

"Hang on high,
For birds to peck as they pass by!"

Seeing a feed room to one side of the barn, the lad slipped within, closing the door behind him. Hardly had this been accomplished than the Negro came forward to take from a nearby peg a set of fine harness for the steed he had been grooming.

"Great Christopher Columbus!" murmured Roger, as he peeped out from a knothole in the door. "A British officer's trappings as sure as fate! I am moving from the frying pan into the fire!"

The horse had been led forward to the doorway, and now the colored man began to buckle on the harness, doing this work within two yards of where Roger stood, scarcely daring to breathe. The operation was nearly completed when there came a cry from outside.

"Cato, is Firefly ready?"

"In a minit, Cap'n," was the answer.

"Get Rosebud ready also—Mr. Bedwell rides with me today."

"Yes, sah."

And then a British captain entered the barn, followed by—Uriah Bedwell.

CHAPTER XXV

A Prisoner Once More

"We must lose no time," said the British captain, as he leaned against the very door behind which Roger was in hiding. "I do not wish to miss the general."

"I trust we find him in good humor, Captain Rembrandt," answered Uriah Bedwell, and now Roger started as he learned whom the British officer was— the same who had escaped from Darrel Kirk's house in Lexington.

"I don't believe we will. He is much cut up over the escape of those two prisoners. He says our prison system must be going to the dogs."

"And what does Howe say?"

"I don't know. He will be in a rage, I expect. Burgoyne was furious."

"And have they no trace of the pair?"

"None whatever. Some marines discovered the man and fired a shot or two after him, down near the burying ground, but young Morse escaped in a very witch like fashion."

"He is a wizard, that boy," growled Bedwell.

"He has caused me no end of trouble. If we—Ha! What is that, a spy?"

The Tory broke off short, as a tremendous sneezing issued from the closet behind Captain Rembrandt.

Some feed had dropped from a shelf to the floor, and the cloud of dust rising up had tickled Roger's nose beyond human endurance. He held back as long as he could, and then let go.

"Ker-chew! Ker-chew! Oh, ker-chew!"

"Somebody is in the closet!" burst from Captain Rembrandt, and wheeling around he threw open the door, and Roger stood revealed.

"Morse, or is it a ghost?" exclaimed Uriah Bedwell. He said ghost, for Roger's clothing was covered with the feed until it was nearly white.

Realizing his position, the youth sought to dart by the two men. But Captain Rembrandt was too quick for him, and hurled him backward, at the same time drawing his pistol.

"Stand where you are, Morse," said the officer. "If you don't I'll put a ball through your head."

"Truly we are in luck!" cried Uriah Bedwell, as soon as he recovered from his astonishment. "Do not let him get away, Captain."

"He won't get away," answered Captain Rembrandt, grimly. "Cato, bring a stout rope. This boy is the one who escaped from the prison last night."

"Is dat so!" gasped the Negro. "He dun be a des'prit character den."

"He is a desperate character," said Bedwell. "Captain, perhaps he is still armed."

"Search him, while I keep him covered."

Very gingerly the Tory approached Roger and felt in the lad's pockets. But the only articles brought to light were the apples taken from Oxley's store.

By this time Cato had procured the rope, and now Roger's hands were bound tightly behind him, and one ankle was tied to the other in such a fashion that he could walk but not run. Uriah Bedwell assisted to make him a close prisoner with keen satisfaction.

"This is the time you have reached the end of your rope, Morse," he said, pursing up his thin lips. "You'll not get away again, I'll warrant."

"And he'll soon dance upon nothing," added Captain Rembrandt, with a coarse laugh.

"I nebber did t'ink dat a boy like dat would kill anybuddy," remarked the colored man.

"Kill anybody?" repeated Roger. "What do you mean? I haven't killed anyone."

"You killed the guard at the prison," observed Captain Rembrandt.

Roger looked from one to the other quickly and gave a gasp. "Is Corporal Grumbert dead?"

"Dead as a doornail—and was that way before you left him."

"But I never touched him. I can swear to that."

"You had better save your words, Morse," said the British captain. "Poor Corporal Grumbert was found with his skull broken from blows with a stone, and you and the other fellow who escaped did the foul deed."

"And you'll hang for it before a week is out," added Uriah Bedwell. "You didn't expect to get caught so quickly, did you? What brought you here to the captain's quarters? It's dangerous ground for a murderer."

"Don't call me a murderer!" burst out Roger, fiercely. "I am willing to fight my enemies, but I never did any underhanded work in my life. If Corporal Grumbert is dead I am not responsible for the deed. My friend loosened the bars on our prison window, and we both got out, and that is all I know about the matter."

"Do you mean to say Grumbert was not on guard?" sneered Captain Rembrandt.

"If he was, I did not see him."

"The other guard can testify against you. You will swing—and so will Conroy—if we can catch him."

At these words, poor Roger's blood seemed to fairly freeze in his veins. He understood only too well now why Conroy had acted in that hurried and peculiar manner. The Connecticut man had taken his revenge upon Grumbert by slaying the corporal, thus opening the way to escape. The prisoners had left together, and now it looked as black for the one as it did for the other.

"I am innocent—I can say no more," said the boy. His heart was too full to utter another word.

"March with me," returned Captain Rembrandt. "We will go into the house first, as I must get those papers for the general."

"Very well," answered Uriah Bedwell. "But keep an eye on him—I would not have him escape for a good deal."

"He shall not escape. Do not fear for it."

"And you will swing!" cried the Tory, pinching Roger's arm. "It will be a sight well worth going to see."

The cut was so severe that the youth could not help resenting it.

"And you shall have your troubles, too, Uriah Bedwell," he burst out, without stopping to think twice. "You expect to swindle Mrs. Alan Brascoe out of her property. Remember that Lieutenant Brascoe left behind him certain papers which—" He stopped short.

"Ha! what do you know of those papers?" burst from the old Tory's lips. "Did you—have you seen them?"

"Never mind."

"Answer my question!" and now Uriah Bedwell caught

Roger by the arm.

"I won't say another word—until the proper time comes. Let go of me."

"You shall speak. Brascoe died behind your orchard wall, and I heard that somebody was found trying to rob him. You must have been that someone."

"What is all this?" put in Captain Rembrandt, curiously.

"This man is a swindler," came from Roger. "He wants to cheat a certain Mrs. Alan Brascoe, widow of a British lieutenant, out of some prop—"

"Hold your tongue!" shouted Bedwell, and clapped his hand over the minute boy's mouth. "There is some mistake here. The boy is laboring under a false impression." He grated his teeth and frowned. "Captain Rembrandt, cannot we—er—cannot we keep him in your house for today?"

"Only for today. I wish to question him. He is a wayward youth, as you know, and if his tongue is allowed to run in public, he may do me much harm. We can turn him over to the authorities tomorrow morning."

"Well, this is a most unusual proceeding, Bedwell. Still, if you desire it—"

"You can place a guard over him, so that escape will be out of the question."

"Very well; I will keep him in the house until tomorrow, and Cato will play guard until that time. Cato, have you your pistol?"

"Yes, sah."

"Then come with us."

Without further words Roger was marched to the mansion in front of the stable. The British captain led the way to an upper side chamber overlooking a narrow alley.

"Let Cato remain on guard, I want to speak to you in private," resumed Uriah Bedwell, whose face showed plainly that he was much troubled.

"Very well," answered Captain Rembrandt. "Cato, is the window locked, as it was when we had that other prisoner here?"

"Yes, sah."

"Then let the boy go, and you remain on guard in the hallway. If he attempts to escape, shoot him on the spot."

"I'll remember dat, sah," was the colored servant's reply. He turned to Roger, "Maybe youse had better recollect dat I kin hit a squirrel at a hundred yahds."

"I can do as much myself," answered the boy, briefly.

His three captors withdrew, locking the door after them, and he was left to himself.

CHAPTER XXVI

The Tory and His Terms

Roger's mind was in a whirl, so rapidly had events moved since his escape from the prison. Here he was a captive once again, and now the awful crime of murder was laid at his door.

"Of course Conroy did the deed," he mused. "But how am I to prove that? He is still free, but even if he is caught, will he admit it? Every man's life is dear to him, and the chances are that Conroy will escape, if such a thing is possible, even if in making the attempt he runs the risk of being shot."

With his heart like a lump of lead within his bosom, the boy sank on a chair in a corner. But he could not remain there long, and springing up, began to pace the floor, nervously.

"What is you up to in dar?" came from Cato, outside.

"I can't sit still," answered the boy. "I must walk around."

"Oh, well, don't yo' go fo' to walk out yere, dat's all," and there followed the click of a pistol hammer.

"I'm not going to walk out there, so don't be alarmed," concluded Roger.

His steps had taken him to the window, a tall, narrow affair, with small panes of glass set in diamond shapes. Looking through these, the lad noted that the alleyway was about eight feet wide, and that the house opposite had several windows close to hand.

"Empty, eh?" he murmured, as he looked into a bare apartment. "I suppose that belongs to some true-hearted man who found Boston too hot to hold him. I wish I could get into the place from here. I might have another chance to escape. But this window is locked, so that scheme is out of the question."

A half hour went by without anybody coming near him. He was now more hungry and thirsty than ever, and started in to question Cato regarding some food, when heavy footsteps sounded outside, the door was flung back, and Uriah Bedwell entered.

"I want to have a talk with you, Morse," began the Tory, after closing the door carefully behind him.

"All right; I am willing, Mr. Bedwell."

"You made a strange statement awhile ago."

"I only spoke the truth."

"I imagine you think you did. You are mistaken, however."

"All right, have it so, if you will," responded Roger, coolly.

"You—ahem—spoke about certain papers—" the Tory paused.

"Exactly."

"Papers that Lieutenant Brascoe left behind him at the time of his death."

"Yes."

"And you said—ahem—something about my— er—my trying to obtain property under false representations."

"I do not know the particulars, Mr. Bedwell, for I am as yet on the outside. When I see Mrs. Brascoe —"

"You will never see her, young man."

"I shall make a strong effort to do so, even if I am placed in prison again."

"Mrs. Brascoe sailed on a transport for England last week."

"Did she, indeed?" And Roger could not help but smile at the barefaced falsehood.

"She did, indeed." Uriah Bedwell saw the smile, and frowned deeply. "Do you doubt my word?"

"I know that what you say is not true."

At this the Tory bit his lip, and began to pace the floor. Suddenly he stopped short.

"You have spoken to her already about this?" he demanded.

"That is my business, sir."

"You refuse to answer my question?"

"Why should I?"

"Why should you? Morse, don't you know that you are in my power? I can shoot you down where you stand if I wish."

"But you won't do it, for you are too afraid of being hung for murder, Uriah Bedwell. Captain Rembrandt may be an enemy, but he won't countenance anything of that sort, and you know it."

"You take too much for granted."

"I know a gentleman when I see one. Captain Rembrandt is all right, even if he is an Englishman, and even though we did have a hot time of it in Lexington. It is his duty to arrest me and bring me before the British authorities, and I am not kicking at it."

"You don't seem to realize your peril. You will be hung for the murder of that prison guard, just as sure as the sun shines."

At these words Roger could not help but shiver, for he felt that that statement, at least, of the Tory was true. Bedwell noted the change with great satisfaction. Suddenly he came quite close to the boy.

"Roger, let us come to terms," he whispered. "I see it is useless to play at hide-and-seek with you. Both of us have much to lose."

"I don't understand what you mean by coming to terms."

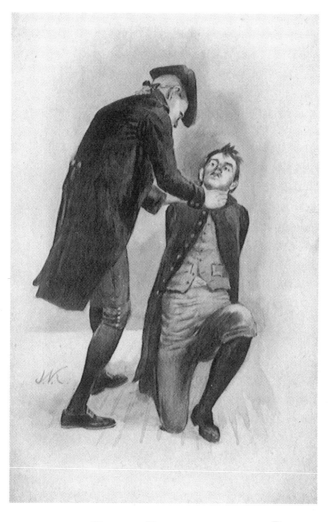

URIAH BEDWELL HURLED HIMSELF UPON THE BOUND AND
DEFENSELESS LAD

"You want to gain your liberty, don't you?"

"Most assuredly."

"Exactly. And I—well, I will be frank—I want to obtain those papers you possess."

"But I haven't owned up that I have them."

"You certainly must have them. Where are they?"

"Safe."

"You haven't them on your person?"

"I have not."

"Where are they?"

"I decline to answer that question."

There was a pause, and Uriah Bedwell took a turn up and down the apartment, his face contracted in deep thought.

"Morse, supposing I should help you to obtain your liberty—help you out of Boston—would that be worth those papers to you?" he asked at last, in low voice.

"You help me to liberty?" cried the youth.

"Yes; help you today, not only to get away from this house, but also to get back into your lines. If I do that, will you turn those papers over to me?"

"You can't help me that far?"

"Yes, I can. Cato can be bribed into letting you get away. Down on the next corner below I will have a carriage in waiting, and a pass to go to Boston Neck can easily be arranged for. I will guarantee you a safe passage into the American camp."

"And the price for all this is to be Mrs. Alan Brascoe's papers—those which prove her right to that property?"

"Yes."

"Mr. Bedwell, I refuse your offer."

"You won't take me up?" cried the Tory, in a rage.

"No, sir, I'll see you in Jericho first."

"Boy, you do not know what you are saying! You stand in the shadow of the gallows."

"Perhaps not. You stand in the shadow of a prison, though."

"Me!"

"Yes, you. Before long Mrs. Brascoe shall know all, and no matter what happens to me, I'll have the satisfaction of knowing that Mr. Uriah Bedwell and Mr. Barnaby Marston have received their just desserts."

With a snarl like that of a wolf Uriah Bedwell hurled himself upon the bound and defenseless lad and bore him to the floor. "I will teach you to defy me!" he foamed. "You—you shall never have the chance to expose me!" and his bony fingers sought Roger's throat.

How far the Tory would have gone it is impossible to say, for at that instant Captain Rembrandt's footsteps sounded out and he was compelled to fall back. "Not a word of this!" he muttered, and then the British officer entered.

"Well, are you finished?" asked the captain of Bedwell.

"Not just yet, Captain. Cannot you allow me another fifteen or twenty minutes?"

"Certainly."

"Captain Rembrandt," broke in Roger. "One word, please."

"What is it?"

"As a prisoner of war I demand protection against this man," and the boy pointed his finger at Uriah Bedwell, who dropped back and looked ready to sink through the floor.

CHAPTER XXVII

In the Deserted Mansion

For a moment there was intense silence, as Captain Rembrandt looked first at Roger and then fastened his gaze upon the shrinking Tory.

"You demand protection?" he said, slowly and doubtfully.

"I do sir. As a prisoner of war I believe I am entitled to fair treatment."

"You are only a rebel prisoner, lad, but you are entitled to fair treatment even at that. What is the trouble?"

"This man wants to—"

"Be still!" shouted Uriah Bedwell, rushing up, but Roger shoved him back.

"Let the boy speak, Bedwell."

"But he wants to—to ruin me. He has always plotted against me," whined Uriah Bedwell. "He is a—a very imp."

"It won't do any harm to hearken to his tale. Why

do you demand protection, Morse?"

"Because this man wants to—to get me out of his way. He is a swindler, and I intend to expose him just as soon as I am in a position to do so."

"A swindler? That is a grave accusation."

"I speak the truth. He is trying to defraud Mrs. Alan Brascoe out of some property."

"Brascoe? You mean Lieutenant Brascoe's widow?"

"Yes, sir."

"What do you know of her property?"

"He knows nothing," interrupted Uriah Bedwell, whose face was as red as a beet. "This is a plot—"

"Captain Rembrant!" The call came from the lower hallway of the mansion. "You are wanted at once. Major Akers is waiting outside."

"The major!" murmured the captain. "I thought it would come." He turned to Roger and the Tory. "I cannot look into this further at present, but I will be back this afternoon. In the meantime, Bedwell, you had better leave, too." The captain called the Negro. "Cato, remain on guard, and see that Morse has a good dinner. And above all, let no one molest him—no one, remember," he added significantly.

"Bedwell said Cato could be bribed," interrupted Roger. "Why not remove me to the regular prison?"

"I will send a guard from there this afternoon or evening. No, Cato is as true as steel. Isn't that so, Cato?"

" 'Deed it am, sah," and the Negro smiled broadly, then turned to frown at Bedwell, who had slunk toward the door. In a moment more the captain and the Tory were gone. The Negro followed them, locking the door as before.

It would be a hard task to analyze Roger's feeling when left alone a second time. He had rejected Bedwell's offer and he wondered what the future held in store for him. Certainly the prospect was not encouraging.

But "while there is life there is hope," and Roger was not one to give way to despondency. He waited until he felt certain the captain and the Tory had left the building, then approached the long, narrow window a second time.

"I could smash this glass with ease," he mused. "But what of the glass opposite? And if I did succeed in smashing that, could I make the leap? It must be ten feet from sill to sill."

His meditations were interrupted by the return of Cato, who was followed by a white girl bearing a tray containing a plate of the ever present pork and beans, some bread and butter, and a saucer of stewed apples, also a small pitcher of water.

"You are very kind," said the boy. "But how am I to eat with my hands bound in this fashion?"

"I will loosen yo' right hand," answered Cato, and did so. "Don't yo' try to escape, boy, or yo' dun git shot, suah," and, with a serious shake of his woolly head, he walked out.

Despite the alarm that filled his breast, Roger ate every mouthful brought to him, washing all down with a generous drink from the pitcher. The meal made him feel much better, and almost immediately he began to form a new plan for escape.

"Supposing I take a nap," he said to Cato, who came in to remove the tray.

"Certainly—sleep as long as yo' please," grinned the Negro. "I ain't gwine to stop yo'," and off he went. At once Roger threw himself on a couch in a corner and closed his eyes.

He had rested thus about a quarter of an hour when the Negro poked his head in to see how matters were going. "Asleep, suah enough," he murmured. He closed the door noiselessly, and listening intently, Roger heard him tiptoe his way along the hall outside and down the stairs.

"Good; that will give me a few minutes, at least," thought the boy, and untying his bonds, he leaped up. Seizing a chair, he stepped toward the window, made a rapid calculation, and struck a heavy blow. A crashing of woodwork and a jingle of glass followed, and so far the way to freedom was cleared.

But this was only the first step. To drop into the alley below and run for it would have been foolhardy.

Still holding the chair, he leaned out of the opening, and aimed a blow at the window opposite. His calculation was true, the chair left his hand to hit the glass and framework squarely, and the article went sailing straight on to the floor beyond.

"Good for that shot!" muttered the minute boy, and stood up in the first window. He made another calculation. A daring leap, and he followed the chair, to land beside it, with nothing more serious as the result of this passage than a scratched left hand from which the blood trickled slowly.

Roger was scarcely safe than he took up the chair and dropped it into the alleyway, directly under the window opposite. Then he brushed the broken glass from the sill before him, so that the damage done in this direction might not be noticed at a glance.

Already was there a commotion in Captain Rembrandt's residence, so the boy felt that if another movement was to be made, the quicker the better.

The apartment he had thus unceremoniously entered was destitute of everything but a large wardrobe, the doors of which stood wide open, showing only empty shelves within. Running to the door of the room, he flung it open, and entered a broad hallway. There were more rooms to the front and the back, and stairs ran up and down.

"I might go down and escape by the rear," he thought,

and started down the stairs. He had just reached the lower landing when he heard loud voices on the street, and soon came the sound of a key being inserted in the huge iron lock of the front door.

With all speed he ran to the rear of the hallway, which was blocked off by the kitchen to the deserted mansion. Here there was a door leading to the yard, but it was locked, and the key was gone. There were also two windows, but each was boarded over to keep out intruders.

"Trapped!" thought the boy; and now his heart sank still more, as he heard the front door flung open and listened to the entrance of Cato and two British soldiers.

"I'll remain on guard here," he heard one of the redcoats say. "Let the Negro go upstairs, and you, Hartpence, can go to the rear," and in a second more the British soldier mentioned was moving toward him.

Like an animal driven to bay, Roger stood in the middle of the kitchen wondering if he could overcome the approaching redcoat. Then of a sudden his eye caught the partly open doorway of a flight of stairs to a cellar. As silently as a shadow he slipped toward it, reached the stairs and closed the door behind him. Then down he flew to the cellar bottom, and hid in the darkest corner to be found, behind a half dozen empty casks.

He heard the tramping of the men overhead as they

moved around from one room to another, and heard Cato go outside to the rear. This lasted for a quarter of an hour, and then a soldier came below, holding up a lantern to light the way.

"If he's here we'll soon have him out," shouted the redcoat to those above, and he moved directly for the spot where poor Roger was in hiding.

CHAPTER XXVIII

ROGER MEETS MRS. ALAN BRASCOE

FOR the moment it looked as if Roger would be discovered, and indeed, the lad gave himself up for lost. The rays of the lantern, however, were dim, and the cellar was consequently still left in semidarkness.

Just in front of Roger was a cask overturned upon its side, resting close to the cellar wall. Crouching down, the minute boy crept into the space left between the wall, the cellar bottom, and the cask, and here he lay scarcely daring to breathe.

"Do you see anything of him, Raymond?" he heard one redcoat ask.

"Not yet," was the answer.

"I don't believe he came down here."

"I'll soon tell you. It's a fine hiding place, and if— What's that?"

A shouting in the street caused the redcoat to break off short.

"Come out! Come out! There is a fellow in the barn in the rear!" came the cry.

"We're on the wrong trail," said the soldier who held the lantern, and he ran for the cellar stairs, closely followed by his companion. Soon they had disappeared, and Roger heard them leave the house.

The minute boy lay quiet for five minutes longer, then arose slowly. The cellar was pitch dark excepting for a faint light which came in through a small side window. This was grated with iron, so escape in that direction was cut off.

"Now, what's to do?" he asked himself, dismally. "They are hunting me as the hounds hunt a fox. I wonder if I hadn't better remain in hiding until tonight?"

He moved around the small cellar with caution, and at last growing bolder, as no one came near the mansion again, he ascended the stairs, to find the door at the top bolted from the other side.

"A prisoner again!" he gasped. He tried to budge the door, but in vain. "Here's a pickle I didn't calculate on."

Finding it utterly impossible to force the door open, he ran down to the cellar bottom once more, and began a tour of inspection. As he felt along the walls, his hand came into contact with many a spider and its web, but undaunted he kept on, until, with great surprise, he reached a latched door. Cautiously he opened it, to find that this gave entrance to a small arched passageway of rough stone. The passageway was nearly a hundred feet in length, and at its further end could be seen a faint streak of light.

"Now where can that lead to?" he thought, and after a slight hesitation moved onward cautiously. Presently, he came to a small flight of stone steps, and ascending these, he entered another cellar, clean, bright, and well-stocked with provisions.

But this cellar, like that just left behind, was well-barred from the outer world, so that escape was again cut off. Yet the door leading to the kitchen was wide open, and from that apartment came the hum of two female voices as their owners rattled among their pots, kettles, and pans.

"He's a fine soldier, even if he is a Yankee," one of the females, a tidy girl of eighteen, was saying. "I never saw a nicer."

"For shame, Lucy!" was the reply, from the other girl. "A Yankee! I hate them worse than ever. See how those two Yankee prisoners murdered poor Corporal Grumbert in cold blood."

"They are not all so bad, Tess."

"No; some are worse," and a vigorous rattle of dishes followed.

The mentioning of Corporal Grumbert gave Roger a cold shiver, and he crouched down in a corner and hardly dared to breathe. Presently the conversation above was continued.

"I don't know what we are coming to, Tess. The whole of Boston can't live like this forever."

"And why not? We have enough to eat and to drink, even though it may not be of the best, and we have a theater open, and the soldiers have their riding school. I don't think poor Lieutenant Brascoe would do it, were he alive."

"Poor man, and the missus crying her eyes out every day because of his death. I caught her crying again only an hour ago, when I took up the coffee."

"She doesn't cry for him alone, Tess, she cries because that Uriah Bedwell is worrying her about something. I hate the sight of that man—he reminds one so much of a snake."

"I agree on that point, Lucy, he is a snake if ever there was one. It's about property, isn't it?"

"I imagine so. Uriah Bedwell was here yesterday, as you know, and as he went out I heard him say something about the land being his, as Mrs. Brascoe would soon learn."

Roger listened to this talk with bated breath. The pair were talking about Mrs. Brascoe. He must be in the widow's house! He could scarcely credit his ears.

The talk ceased, and in a minute after the girl Lucy came tripping down into the cellar for some potatoes.

The barrel stood in the very corner where Roger was hiding, and as she tipped it over she could not help but see him.

"Mercy!" she gasped, and was on the point of screaming, when he clapped his hand over her mouth.

"Don't make a noise," he commanded, in a low tone. "Keep quiet."

"But—but—who are you?" she stammered, when he let her speak.

"Never mind who I am; answer my questions. Is this Mrs. Alan Brascoe's home?"

"Yes, sir."

"Does she live here alone?"

"Oh, no, there are several families of British officers live here."

"But she has her private apartments?"

"Oh, yes."

"Is she alone now?"

"She is, sir."

"I am glad to hear that." Roger thought for a moment. "You work for the lady?"

"I work for three ladies—wives of the officers."

"Would you like to do Mrs. Brascoe a good turn?"

"To be sure, sir. But—but—"

"Then listen to me. Go to her and tell her that I am here, and tell her that I carry a message from her husband, who was killed at Lexington. I would like to see her in private, and tell her that I trust, for her husband's sake, she will not expose my presence here to anyone."

"And do you really bring a message from the dear dead lieutenant?" asked the working girl, in curiosity.

"I do. Now go, and don't tell a soul but Mrs. Brascoe that I am here."

The girl departed immediately, and closed the cellar door after her. A quarter of an hour went by, a time which to Roger just then appeared an age. What would be the outcome of this strange adventure?

The door opened and the girl Lucy reappeared. "Come with me, quick!" she whispered. "Tess has gone to the barn, and Mrs. Brascoe is waiting for you in her dressing room."

At once he followed the girl up through the kitchen, across a wide hallway and to an upper apartment luxuriously furnished.

"Here he is, madam," said Lucy, and showed him within, and Roger was left alone with the lady he had hoped so many times to meet.

He found the widow a small, beautiful lady of thirty-five. Her face was pale and full of a sorrow that went straight to his youthful heart. She stood in the center of the room, and as he came forward she stepped toward him impulsively.

"You—you bring me a message?" she faltered.

"If you are Mrs. Brascoe, the widow of Lieut. Alan Bascoe, I do," said Roger. And as she bowed, he continued. "I was with the brave lieutenant when he— he breathed his last."

"Yes?" She wiped her eyes and motioned him to a seat beside her on a couch. "And what were his last words, pray?"

"His last words were, 'Tell my wife that I died as a soldier.'" To repeat that sentence nearly choked Roger as he saw how deeply the woman beside him was affected. "But he had other things to tell, and he left in my keeping a packet of documents, relating, I believe, to some property belonging to you."

"Those documents! Is it possible? Thank Heaven they are come to light! You—you have them with you?"

"I have not. But they are safe at my home at Lexington. There are three papers, drawn up by a lawyer named Charles Wilburton, and signed by one Alan Brascoe and several others."

"They are the papers—and I—my claim is safe. But how came you here? Why, you are but a boy!"

"The story is rather a long one, madam. Can I trust you to keep my secret?"

"Yes; for you have been a friend, even though an enemy."

"I am not *your* enemy," he answered, and, without hesitation, told his tale just as I have narrated it in the foregoing pages. The widow listened without a word, but when he was done she caught both of his hands.

"You poor boy, how you have suffered!" she said. "I believe you when you say you had nothing to do with the murder of Corporal Grumbert. If it is possible to do so, I will see to it that you are returned to the American lines in safety. But we must be careful, or—"

A knock on the door interrupted the conversation.

"Mr. Bedwell and Mr. Marston to see you, Mrs. Brascoe," announced a servant, and Roger leaped up in consternation.

CHAPTER XXIX

OPERATIONS DURING THE SIEGE

"THOSE men!" cried the boy. "What shall I do?"

"I will go below and see them. You can remain here," answered Mrs. Brascoe. "Do not fear—I will never betray you. But I am glad I can dare Uriah Bedwell to do his worst, I can tell you that."

In a minute more she left the room and descended to a parlor on the ground floor. Left alone Roger gave himself up to his thoughts. His mind was easier than it had been for many hours, for Mrs. Brascoe had promised to help him, and he felt sure she would be able to do a great deal.

Half an hour had gone by, when, without warning, Roger saw the door flung open and a richly attired elderly lady tripped into the dressing room. "Mrs. Brascoe, I am going—" she began, then stopped short, and stared at Roger in astonishment. "Robbers! Thieves! Watch! Watch!" she screamed, and ran out into the hallway before Roger could make the first movement to stop her. Her own room was just across from Mrs. Brascoe's apartment, and here sat her husband reading a book. "Henry, go quickly, there is a robber here!" she went on, and Captain Henry Becket, the man who had escaped from Lexington months before, leaped up, pistol in hand.

In a moment more the entire mansion was in commotion, and half a dozen women and officers were running to the room where Roger was seeking vainly for a hiding place. Soon he was dragged out into the hallway and to a large window.

"The boy that escaped after murdering Corporal Grumbert!" cried one of the officers. "This is a fine haul, indeed!"

"A murderer!" shrieked the richly attired lady. "Oh, Henry, save us all!" And then she fainted dead away.

While Roger was being made a close prisoner, Mrs. Brascoe came up, followed by Uriah Bedwell and Deacon Marston.

"That boy!" gasped the old Tory. Then he turned to the lady. "Now, I understand it all. So he came to you after his escape from me? He shall suffer dearly for his atrocious crime!"

"And so they have discovered you—too bad!" said Mrs. Brascoe to Roger, and she looked at him pityingly.

"Did you actually harbor this—this young villain?"

put in the captain, turning quickly to the widow.

"He is no villain—only a plain prisoner of war, Captain Becket. He was my late husband's friend."

"She is in league with the rascal," burst out Uriah Bedwell. "She—she ought to be put into prison with him." The failure of his schemes had driven him wild. "Arrest her, Captain, by all means."

"If you were sheltering this escaped prisoner, Mrs. Brascoe, I cannot do less than ask you to accompany us to the Court House, where the lad and yourself will have a hearing," said Captain Becket, after a painful pause.

"Very well; I will go," announced Mrs. Brascoe, quietly.

"This is infamous—" began Roger, when he was silenced.

"Do your talking at the prison," said an officer. "You are badly wanted there. I know this boy is a deep one."

Half an hour later found Roger at the substantial stone and brick building which was used as both a court house and prison. Here he was given a brief hearing, and then led away to a cell in the rear. The hearing then proceeded, and Mrs. Brascoe was also detained at the prison.

Several days went by, and nobody but a jailer came to see the boy, and he had but little to say and was always on his guard. "He thinks I murdered that other fellow and may murder him," thought Roger, with a shudder.

At the end of a week a lawyer came to him. "You are accused of a grave crime, Morse," he said. "You will come up for trial soon. I have been assigned to defend you."

"Has Conroy been caught yet?" asked Roger, eagerly. "No."

"And the authorities feel sure I took Grumbert's life?"

"It looks that way. Of course, we can set up the strongest defense possible, my lad," went on Aaron Carson, for such was the lawyer's name.

"Is Mrs. Brascoe still here?"

"Yes. She is charged with aiding you to escape."

"And I suppose Uriah Bedwell is doing his best to press both the charge against me and against her," added the minute boy, bitterly.

"I must confess that he is—he and a man named Marston. They seem very bitter against you."

Roger was to stand trial in less than a month, and Aaron Carson wanted to get all of the evidence possible in his favor. But Roger could scrape up no witness in his behalf, so but little could be done.

"I seem to be worse off than ever," he mused, when left alone. "Oh, if they should hang me for that murder! What will Mother and Dorothy say?" And he could not restrain his tears. By Mr. Carson's aid he tried to get a letter through the lines to his folks. The communication passed Boston Neck, but strange as it may seem, it was never delivered.

Slowly the days dragged along after this. In the meantime, Washington and his army still lay about Cambridge, Charlestown Neck, and behind Dorchester, with strong fortifications at Prospect Hill, Winter Hill, and other points, fortifications which were being increased almost weekly. "We are hedged in, we cannot escape," murmured more than one redcoat. Howe, who had superseded Gage in command, and the higher officers said nothing, but, doubtless, they were doing a good bit of thinking.

Our commander-in-chief now had the army in good condition, but powder was still a scarce article, and without this but little could be accomplished. All of the colonies were called upon in secret to contribute to the general store, but they could send very little, for the war was breaking out at other points: Crown Point and Ticonderoga, attacked even before the battle of Bunker Hill; the advance upon Canada at Montreal and Quebec, and the reduction of Falmouth (now Portland) by a British ship of war. An expedition also went to Long Island in whaleboats, but little came of it.

New Year's Day, 1776, had been one which no

American should ever forget, for on that day the glorious stars and stripes of our beloved country was first thrown to the breeze. Heretofore the colonists had used the pine tree flag, the rattlesnake flag and several others, but now it was to be the inspiring stars and stripes for evermore.

Early in February a skirmish had occurred on Main Street, near Charlestown Neck. A few houses here had escaped the conflagration at the time of the battle of Bunker Hill, and General Putnam started out to destroy them. A sharp fight ensued, and the whole of Boston was thrown into a panic, thinking an assault had begun. This panic spread to the theater, where a humorous play called the "Blockade of Boston" was in progress. An actor was just trying to make Washington ridiculous when there came the cry: "The enemy! Officers, to your posts!" and a number of ladies fainted.

In this same month Washington's army was greatly strengthened by the addition of several fresh regiments of soldiers. From Crown Point and Ticonderoga, Colonel Knox brought down to his chief over fifty cannon, mortars, and howitzers, and also some much needed powder. It was now decided that Washington should take possession of Dorchester Heights, and plant there a battery that would place Boston at the Americans' mercy. This work must be done ere spring should arrive and Howe could obtain reinforcements from England.

The movement began on Monday, the fourth of March. At night a fierce cannonading was begun, and while the British attention was attracted by this, General Thomas, with two thousand men and with carts and entrenching tools, moved toward Dorchester Heights. With these troops were Dick, Paul, Ben, and a number of the other minute boys, and also Mr. Winthrop and Mr. Small. Mr. Cresson had not yet returned to the army, nor had poor Hen, who was still hovering between life and death.

Never did boys and men work more diligently than upon that night. The moon shone brightly, and from a distance came the cannonading that was covering up the real movement of the colonists. At first great bales of hay were strung along Dorchester Neck, and by the time the sun arose on the morning following, two forts were so far advanced that they could easily withstand anything but very heavy cannon shots.

The astonishment of the British was beyond description. "The rebels have done more in one night than my whole army would have done in a month," wrote General Howe. "It must have been the employment of at least twelve thousand men."

Arrangements were at once made to move against the Americans, just as the redcoats had moved against them at Bunker Hill. For this purpose a number of transports were brought into use and filled with British soldiers. Washington heard of the proposed attack, and lost no time in strengthening his lines. "Remember, soldiers," he said, on the fifth of March, "it is the anniversary of the Boston Massacre, and avenge your brethren." The troops cheered wildly and promised to do their best.

But the expected conflict did not come off, for on that day, and for several days following, the wind blew so strongly and the sea ran so high that no small boat could live in it, and the British soldiers were compelled to remain in Boston. The Neck was completely submerged, the water dashing high over meadow and causeway. In the meantime Washington strengthened his position, until to take it would have cost even a larger sacrifice of life than had the taking of Breed's and Bunker Hills.

General Howe's situation now became truly desperate. The Americans with their cannon commanded the town, and the British ships were unable to ride in safety in the harbor. To remain in Boston seemed out of the question, and to get out to fight the ever increasing army of the colonies would be taking a tremendous risk, for, if defeat followed, the British troops would all be killed or taken prisoners. He had received word that he might leave Boston, and now he resolved to evacuate as gracefully but as speedily as possible.

The news that the British troops were going away

filled the Americans with joy, but it brought consternation to the Tory, and among these hot-tempered ones were Uriah Bedwell and Barnaby Marston. As the preparations to evacuate progressed the Tories became utterly lawless, and aided by the soldiers and the sailors from the warships, they broke open the houses and the stores, and confiscated everything of value that could conveniently be carried away. What some of these operations led to we will see in the chapter to follow.

CHAPTER XXX

"How long is this to last? It seems to me I shall go crazy, one day is so much like another."

It was Roger who spoke, as he paced the narrow confines of his prison cell. Weeks had passed since he had been placed there, yet nothing had been done toward bringing him to trial. Mr. Carson had tried several times to have the case brought up, but had failed. The prisoner was but a boy, let him wait, the crown had matters of more importance demanding its attention.

Mrs. Brascoe was likewise a prisoner, and once in a great while the pair had been allowed to communicate with each other. Both were suffering from poor food and the want of fresh air, and the lady looked as if she might go into a permanent decline at any moment.

Once Uriah Bedwell had called upon Roger, and tried to learn something about where the documents belonging to Mrs. Brascoe had been placed. But the minute boy had refused to talk to the Tory, much to the man's rage. "All right; wait, I'll fix you yet!" had been Bedwell's threat upon parting.

For several days Roger had noted that something unusual was in the air. Time and again he had heard heavy firing, and wondered how the tide of the contest was turning, but his jailer gave him no information, falling continually back upon the old saying, "Ask me no questions and I'll tell you no lies." But that the jailer was much worried there could be no doubt.

One night the boy could not sleep. From afar came the booming of cannon, and he kept wondering if his chums were still fighting, and if Hen Peabody was dead or alive. At last resting became out of the question, and he arose and began to walk up and down. When he halted it was in front of the cell door, and now to his amazement he saw that the door was unlocked!

"Gracious!" came to his lips, but he checked himself and caught hold of the door. It swung open with ease, and in an instant he was out in the long, gloomy corridor. Not a soul was in sight. Like a phantom he glided down the corridor to a rear door, unlocked this, and passed into the night air.

All was dark, for the moon had gone under a heavy cloud. On he sped, not knowing in what direction he was going, and caring little, if only that awful jail might be left behind. Passing through an alleyway he crossed a crooked street, and dove into another alleyway, between a silversmithing establishment and a linen draper's shop. Here in the intense darkness he paused for breath and to collect his somewhat bewildered thoughts.

He was free! But where should he go? He was still in the town of his enemies, and the coming of daylight would make it almost impossible for him to hide—he knew that from former experiences.

Suddenly footsteps sounded upon the pavements. A band of half drunken sailors were coming along, led by a boatswain as tipsy as his men.

"Here's another linen draper's!" roared the seafaring man. "Burst open the door, lads, and out with the cloth! We have no time to lose. Orders are to leave nothing behind for those rebels."

"Here's a silversmith's, Dicket!" cried one of the sailors. "A crib wuth crackin'. Wot say, chaps? A golden mug for all hands?"

"Right ye be, Ugly Pete!" came from half a dozen voices. "The linin can wait, eh, mates?"

And then came another rush, followed by a tremendous crash, as the shuttered door of the silversmith's place was driven in. Then in went the crowd, pell-mell, each man swinging a ship's lantern over his arm, and pocketing or bagging whatever came to his hands.

"They are looting the town!" thought Roger. "That

means something. Can the British be on the point of leaving?"

The sailors had been in the silversmith's place but a few minutes when along the pavements came another crowd of men, soldiers and Tories.

"A crowd is ahead of us!" came the cry. "What does this mean? Who gave the orders for you to come here?"

"I want my plate!" shrieked out a thin voice, and Roger held his breath as he recognized the voice of Uriah Bedwell.

"Your plate?" said another. "I thought your plate was confiscated by the rebels."

"Part of it was, but—"

A confusion of voices drowned out the remainder of the Tory's words, and then came cries and vile exclamations as the soldiers and Tories tried to drive the sailors away. Crack! Crack! Two pistol shots rang out, and a yell of pain followed. "Guard! Watch!" bawled somebody. "I am shot!" Then the confusion became even greater than before, and a dozen pistol shots rent the midnight air.

Roger was too interested to move, wondering what Uriah Bedwell was doing there, and how he was faring. The strife continued; but in a few minutes the sailors came running out into the street, and as a dozen additional soldiers put in an appearance, they took to their heels and disappeared in the direction of the shipping.

"To your barracks, men!" came the command from a captain of grenadiers. "There is not a moment to lose. Wind and tide willing, we leave Boston tomorrow morning."

A shout went up, but it was some time before the soldiers left the establishment. "These gentlemen want everything," sneered one, referring to the Tories. "I trust you enjoy yourselves when the rebels come in."

"I shall go to England with you," cried one Tory. "I will not remain behind to be humiliated."

"We will burn the tower first," added another.

"Do it, and General Howe will order the rebels to hang you," was the mocking return, and then the two parties separated.

From the silversmithing establishment, the Tories went to the linen draper's shop. But here nothing of value was left, for the proprietor had sold out a month before. In the meantime, one man remained out on the pavement, nursing a wounded arm. It was Uriah Bedwell.

"Bedwell, where are you?" came in Barnaby Marston's voice. "I heard you were shot."

"It is not so bad as I supposed," answered Bedwell, as Marston came up. "Is it true General Howe leaves tomorrow?"

"So I have been told."

"It is hard." Uriah Bedwell grated his teeth. "We are foiled at every point. Marston, I shall join the firebrands without delay."

"I am with you. I hate Boston and all in it."

"You do? Then come with me. But we must be careful. Come." And the two men moved off.

Roger had listened to every word. The news filled him with astonishment, joy, and fear. The enemy was going to leave! But what if the noble old town was laid in ashes?

"It must not be," he muttered. "I will follow them and see what they do."

On he went, less than fifty feet behind the pair. A corner was passed, and they turned into a street which was little better than a lane. As Roger followed, he fell headlong over the body of a drunken sailor, sleeping with his feet against the steps to a house.

The sailor did not awaken more than to grunt out half a dozen unintelligible words; and as Roger fell, his hand touched the man's pistol. Instantly he appropriated the weapon, and also the fellow's cap, bearing the name *Wicklow*.

Bedwell had passed into another house a hundred feet farther on, and Marston had followed. All had been dark, but as the boy came up the flash of a lantern lit up the pavement.

"Ha! Who is this?" came from the hallway of the

house. "That Morse boy, as I live!" And Uriah Bedwell came out again.

"Morse, true enough!" exclaimed Marston. "Capture him! Watch, ho, watch! An escaped prisoner!"

Both Tories made a leap for Roger and bore him to the ground. A fierce struggle followed, in the midst of which the boy's pistol was discharged. The flash of fire crossed Marston's cheek, and the bullet entered Bedwell's shoulder.

Two yells of pain told that the shot had been effective, and Roger leaped back and set off on a run. Soon he reached another street, and turning a corner, made for the shipping. He heard the crowd coming after him, and ran faster than ever.

The wharves reached, he found all in confusion; for soldiers, sailors, and marines were everywhere, getting ready to leave. The streets and the docks were piled high with merchandise and military stores, more twice over than all of the vessels under General Howe's command could carry. In this confusion it was an easy matter for him to escape notice.

The night that followed was one Roger never forgot. When day dawned all was still in confusion. But the British troops had abandoned Bunker Hill and their other defenses, and they must be off. At last, one ship after another began to sail, until the harbor was alive with them. From a loft overlooking the shipping the minute boy saw everything, but took the best of care not to expose himself. The British sailed for Halifax, and the long siege of Boston was over. Within twenty-four hours afterward, Boston was in possession of the Americans, to remain their own to the present day.

CHAPTER XXXI

Home Once More—Conclusion

"Mother, the British have evacuated Boston!"

"Can that news be true, Dorothy?" asked Mrs. Morse. "Remember, General Howe has a strong army there."

"Mr. Winthrop just brought the news. General Putnam is marching into the town and occupying all of the important fortifications."

"Heaven be praised for that!" murmured Mrs. Morse. Then her face clouded. "Poor, dear Roger, how I wish he had lived to enjoy this day!" And she wiped the tears from her eyes, while Dorothy turned away to dry her own cheeks.

A tall, pale, feeble looking man hobbled in. "Wot's this news, Miss Dorothy?" he asked. "Them air Britishers hev got out, you say?"

"Yes, Hen, they have sailed, bag and baggage."

"Glory tew Peter! Gosh, but thet's prime news now, ain't it?" and the hired man shook his head enthusiastically. "Wisht I was thar tew hev seen 'em go. I would most hev danced a jig o' j'y, yes, I would!"

"A good many of our men and boys were there, so Mr. Winthrop was telling me," went on the girl. "It must have been a great time all around. The whole army will be allowed to go into the town as soon as the smallpox has been taken care of, so he said."

"It's a great victory fer General Washington," was Hen's comment. "Reckon them air redcoats think we are of sum account—now," he added, with emphasis.

Mrs. Morse had moved toward the window, glancing out carelessly. But now a familiar figure on the highway from Boston caught her eye, and made her straighten up. "Oh, pray Heaven it is he!" she burst out.

"He? Who, Mother?"

"It is—yes—oh, Dorothy, do I see aright? tell me quickly!" And Mrs. Morse's breath came so rapidly she could scarcely speak.

The daughter gave one swift glance. "Roger! He is alive! Roger! Oh, Mother!" And then she flew for the doorway and out of the house, with Mrs. Morse and Hen coming after. All three gained the gateway as Roger entered it.

"My son! My son!" Mrs. Morse could say no more, but fell fainting in his arms. Dorothy was all in a tremble and shed tears of joy, while Hen and Roger were no less affected.

"We all thought you dead," said the hired man. "It's like as if you had come back from the grave."

"Then you didn't get my letter? I thought it strange I never heard a word from any of you," answered the boy, and then he carried his mother into the house and placed her on a couch. She quickly recovered and a general rejoicing followed. Soon the neighbors heard of Roger's homecoming and flocked in to shake him by the arm. Nellie heard of it, too, and came with her father. Roger saw this one particular friend in private, and although no outsider knows just what was said at the time, certain it is that both looked far happier than ever before when the greeting was over.

Here I must bring to a close this tale of *The Minute Boys of Bunker Hill* and of scenes and incidents connected with the siege of Boston. The British had left the vicinity not to return, and for the time being the colonists in and about the town were secured against additional trouble and bloodshed. The work of minutemen and minute boys was over, and they were privileged to return to their homes or join the regular army, as they saw fit.

Roger was anxious to learn what had become of Mrs. Brascoe, and as soon as he could he returned to Boston, taking with him the precious packet of papers. He found that the lady had been released and had retired into the family of one of the colonists. By means of the documents Roger had saved she was enabled to prove her claim to property worth many thousands of pounds sterling, and as a reward she turned over to Roger the deed of some Massachusetts land, upon which the minute boy later on settled down to live, with sweet Nellie Winthrop as his wife.

At first nothing could be learned concerning Conroy, but later on it leaked out that he had sailed on a coastwise vessel for New York. The man had often boasted of killing the prison guard single handed, so Roger's name was cleared of this crime, if crime it can be justly called.

Uriah Bedwell and Deacon Marston had lost both their reputations and their wordly goods, and when they left their beds of sickness neither had a friend to whom to apply for assistance. In the end Marston became little better than a beggar around Boston, and spent the last year of his life in the poorhouse. Uriah Bedwell secured a small loan from some relatives of his wife, and with this money removed himself and his family to New York, there to begin again, in a humble way, his practice of the law.

Many of the minute boys joined the regular army during the early part of 1776, but for the present Roger had seen enough of the struggle and he felt that he was needed at home fully as much as on the battlefield. Mrs. Morse's health was far from even fair, and he could not bear to think of her dying when he was not at her side.

"I will remain, Mother," he whispered, as he stroked her hair fondly. "You know you are all the mother I have."

"And you are my only son," she answered. And then as she heaved a long sigh, she murmured: "How like his father he is growing!"

"We can't have you go, Roger," was what Dorothy said. "Remember, you have been away from us for nearly a year."

"I shall never forget it," he answered, gravely. "A year! And the greater part of the time was spent in prison! To my mind prison life is worse than life on the battlefield," and there the subject was dropped; and here we will take leave of our hero and all of the others, wishing them well.

THE END

GLOSSARY

——+——

afforded af-ford´-ed *verb* provided or gave *18*

annihilation an-ni-hi-la´-tion *noun* complete destruction *190*

apothecary shop a-poth´-e-car-y shop *noun* store of a druggist or
pharmacist *199*

appease ap-pease´ *verb* pacify or quiet down *77*

artillery ar-til´-ler-y *noun* cannons and other big guns *172, 173, 184*

ascertained as-cer-tained´ *verb* found out for sure *17, 156*

assaulting as-sault´-ing *noun* attacking or fighting *48*

attendant at-tend´-ant *adjective* following or going along with as a
result *164*

avail a-vail´ *verb* to be of use *55, 177*

axe to grind axe to grind *phrase* to have a goal of one's own to meet or
gain *38*

bated breath bat´-ed breath *phrase* not daring to breath out loud for fear
or excitement *274*

batteries bat´-ter-ies *noun* the place where heavy guns are placed
157, 168, 182

besieged be-sieged´ *adjective* hemmed in by armed forces; under
attack *36, 146*

betook be-took´ *verb* went *103*

biers biers *noun* platforms on which coffins rest *229*

blind blind *noun* something which misleads or deceives someone *243*

boatswain boat´-swain *noun* ship's officer in charge of the crew, the rigging, the anchors, and so on *290*

breastworks breast´-works *noun* low walls put up quickly for defense *152, 157, 158*

brethren breth´-ren *noun* brothers *286*

brig brig *noun* prison *79*

broadside broad´-side *noun* the firing of all the guns on one side of a ship at the same time *159, 160, 161*

bump of inquisitiveness bump of in-quis´-i-tive-ness *phrase* curiosity; desire to find things out *115*

bung bung *noun* a cork or stopper used to stop up a hole *25, 30, 31*

bunghole bung´-hole *noun* a hole in a keg through which the contents may be emptied out *25*

cannonading can-non-ad´-ing *verb* attacking by firing cannons *108, 168, 171*

cataract cat´-a-ract *noun* large waterfall *189*

cavalry cav´-al-ry *adjective* troops which ride on horseback *32, 63*

chagrin cha-grin´ *noun* embarrassment or annoyance *151*

chain shot chain shot *noun* a cannon shot made of two balls connected with a chain, mainly used to destroy masts on a ship *167*

channel chan´-nel *noun* deeper part of a body of water *65*

circular letter cir´-cu-lar let´-ter *noun* leaflet or letter intended to be passed around to as many people as possible *59*

close close *adjective* guarded carefully *43, 250*

coastwise coast´-wise *adjective* along or near the coast *299*

cocks of hay cocks of hay *noun* small, rounded piles of hay *63, 70*

commissary department com´-mis-sar-y de-part´-men *noun* military store where food and supplies are kept *203*

Common Com´-mon *noun* piece of land in a town for public use *58*

concoction con-coc´-tion *noun* something made by mixing several things together *200*

condign con-dign´ *adjective* deserved or suitable *150*

confederate con-fed´-er-ate *noun* someone who works with one for a common purpose *122*

confiscate con´-fis-cate *verb* seize; take by force *16*

conflagration con-fla-gra´-tion *noun* a large fire *178, 284*

consternation con-ster-na´-tion *noun* fear or shock that leaves one helpless or not knowing what to do *278, 287*

Continental army Con-ti-nen´-tal ar´-my *noun* American army *147, 202*

countenance coun´-te-nance *verb* give approval to; allow *258*

crow crow *verb* boast *90*

cupola cu´-po-la *noun* a dome-like structure on the top of a building *214, 215*

cut up cut up *verb phrase* upset; distressed *248*

decline de´-cline *noun* failing of health *288*

deep potion deep po´-tion *noun* a great or large drink *41*

demurred de-murred´ *verb* hesitated or had doubts about *187, 195*

despatched des-patched´ *verb* finished off quickly *113*

despondency de-spond´-en-cy *noun* loss of hope or courage *266*

detachment de-tach´-ment *noun* a small unit of troops, organized for a special mission *16, 17*

detained de-tained´ *verb* kept back *108*

Devon farmer Dev´-on farm´-er *noun* farmer from the county of Devon, in southwest England *44*

dilapidated di-lap´-i-dat-ed *adjective* run-down or falling to pieces *27, 133*

discharged dis´-charged *verb* fired or shot *53*

discomfited dis-com´-fit-ed *verb* made uncomfortable *163*

disdained dis-dained´ *verb* regarded with contempt; looked down upon *66*

disheartened dis-heart´-ened *adjective* lost courage; discouraged *195*

dispatched dis-patched´ *verb* eaten up quickly *130, 158*

distinguished dis-tin´-guished *verb* seen clearly *72*

do us foul do us foul *verb phrase* harm us; kill us *35*

draw rein draw rein *verb phrase* pull back on the horse's rein to make it stop *50*

earthworks earth´-works *noun* walls or fortifications made by piling up earth *152, 160*

embarking em-bark´-ing *verb* going aboard a ship *170*

eminence em´-i-nence *noun* hill *171*

entrenching en-trench´-ing *noun* the digging of a trench or ditch *155*

ere ere *preposition* before *199, 222*

evacuate e-vac´-u-ate *verb* leave or withdraw *286, 287*

famine fam´-ine *noun* extreme lack of food causing starvation *62*

fervently fer´-vent-ly *adverb* in a manner showing great feeling *227*

field pieces field piec´-es *noun* movable cannons used on a battlefield *102, 103, 173*

firebrands fire´-brands *noun* those who stir others to revolt;
revolutionaries *293*

flatiron crowbar flat´-i-ron crow´-bar *noun* a long, iron tool used to pry
open boxes *37*

flint and steel flint and steel *noun* pieces of rock and steel which make
sparks when struck together *24, 39, 44*

flintlock musket flint´-lock mus´-ket *noun* an older gun than the rifle, it
used a hammer to strike a metal plate, making a spark, thereby
causing gunpowder to explode *20, 22, 50*

flip flip *noun* a sweet drink of beer, wine or liquor made with eggs
and spices *79*

flood tide flood tide *noun* the incoming, rising tide *64, 168*

fodder fod´-der *noun* rough food for animals to eat, like hay or straw *35*

forenoon fore´-noon *noun* morning *168*

forsook for-sook´ *verb* abandoned, left *193, 205*

fortifications for-ti-fi-ca´-tions *noun* things which strengthen or help to
defend a position *63, 296*

furloughs fur´-loughs *noun* time off from service *148, 152*

gained gained *verb* reached or arrived at *50, 72, 189*

galling gall´-ing *adjective* irritating or annoying *177*

garrisoned gar´-ri-soned *verb* placed troops in a fortified place to
defend it *203*

gill gill *noun* a measure equal to 4 ounces *168*

grape grape *noun* a group of small iron balls fired from a cannon *164, 171*

grated grat´-ed *verb* framed with metal bars *272*

grenadiers gren-a-diers´ *noun* members of a special regiment of the
army, armed with grenades *172, 173, 182*

gruel gru´-el *noun* watered-down porridge or cooked cereal *12, 13*

gunwale gun´-wale *noun* the upper edge of the side of a boat or ship *90*

hamlet ham´-let *noun* small village *59*

harboring the enemy har´-bor-ing the en´-e-my *verb phrase* hiding the
enemy *17*

hearken heark´-en *verb* listen; hear *264*

hermetically sealed her-met´-i-cal-ly sealed *adjective* closed so that no
air may get in *229*

high dudgeon high dudg´-eon *noun* extremely angry *221*

homestead farm home´-stead farm *noun* family farm, includes house,
land and any outbuildings *15, 42*

howitzers how´-itz-ers *noun* a short cannon, slightly larger than a
mortar *284*

humor hu´-mor *noun* mood; state of mind *197*

hypocrite hyp´-o-crite *noun* one who pretends to be something other
than what he is *17, 98, 99*

in trust in trust *phrase* in the condition of being given to someone else's care *48*

Indian file In´-di-an file *noun* single file, one person following the other *44*

infamous in´-fa-mous *adjective* outrageous; disgraceful *281*

infantry in´-fan-try *noun* soldiers that fight on foot *172, 173, 182*

infernal regions in-fer´-nal re´-gions *noun* hell *53*

injunction in-junc´-tion *noun* command or order *48*

inquisitive in-quis´-i-tive *adjective* questioning; prying *40*

insignia in-sig´-ni-a *noun* badges or emblems *203*

iron foundry i´-ron found´-ry *noun* place where iron is melted down and cast into molds *213*

jackstraws jack´-straws *verb* long, narrow strips of wood used in a game *118*

jig will be up jig will be up *phrase* all chances for success will be gone *75*

just desserts just des-serts´ *noun* a deserved ending *262*

latchstring latch´-string *noun* a string attached to the latch on a door inside a house, which raises the latch when pulled from the outside *136*

lay lay *noun* story or song *80*

lief lief *adverb* gladly; willingly *221, 245*

lighter light´-er *noun* an open barge used to load and unload ships in a harbor *64*

linen draper's shop lin´-en drap´-er's shop *noun* shop where fine cloth is sold *290, 292*

loath loath *adjective* unwilling, reluctant *190*

loiterers loi´-ter-ers *noun* person who stands around with no purpose *236*

man-of-war man-of-war *noun* armed warship *66, 69, 71*

marine glass ma-rine´ glass *noun* telescope used on the sea *70*

martial law mar´-tial law *noun* governing of the citizens in a town by the military authorities *150*

meditatingly med-i-ta´-ting-ly *adverb* thinking deeply *120*

meetinghouse meet´-ing-house *noun* building used for worship or meetings *21, 131*

minuteman min´-ute-man *noun* armed, American, male citizen who has promised to be ready to fight at a minute's notice *11, 32*

mortars mor´-tars *noun* a cannon with a short barrel *284*

nasal organ na´-sal or´-gan *noun* nose *115*

nerved nerved *verb* gave strength or courage to *185*

noncombatant non-com-ba´-tant *noun* civilian; one who does not fight *41*

Old Nick Old Nick *noun* the devil *141*

outworks out´-works *noun* the defenses, usually trenches, built out beyond the main fortifications *156*

pantry pan´-try *noun* small room off the kitchen, used for storage *121*

parapet par´-a-pet *noun* low wall, screening troops from enemy fire *189, 190*

Parliament Par´-lia-ment *noun* legislative branch of the government of Great Britain *48*

pell mell pell mell *adverb* without any order *185, 290*

peninsula pen-in´-su-la *noun* piece of land which extends out into the water *152, 195*

picket guard pick´-et guard *noun* soldiers posted to guard *94, 155*

pikemen pike´-men *noun* soldiers carrying pikes *22*

pikes pikes *noun* weapons made by attaching a metal spearhead to a wooden shaft *22*

pillory pil´-lo-ry *noun* a punishment device which used a wooden board with holes for the head and hands, in which the person was locked up *215*

pippins pip´-pins *noun* apples *237*

pitch pitch *noun* tar or asphalt *24*

piteously pit´-e-ous-ly *adverb* in a way that causes pity *179*

pitfalls pit´-falls *noun* dangers or trouble that lay ahead *154*

plate plate *noun* dishes and utensils made of silver or gold *38, 39*

plowshares plow´-shares *noun* sharp, cutting part of a plow *131*

poorhouse poor´-house *noun* a home for poor people paid for with public money *299*

pothouse pot´-house *noun* tavern *237*

pounds sterling pounds ster´-ling *noun* basic unit of British money, a pound was worth 20 shillings *299*

powderhorns pow´-der-horns *noun* containers made from the horns of a cow or ox and used to carry gunpowder *40*

prime prime *adjective* primary or main; best *17, 296*

procured pro-cured´ *verb* obtained; gotten *55, 250*

proffers prof´-fers *noun* attempts; offers *55*

prostrate pros´-trate *adverb* lying face down *185*

provender prov´-en-der noun food *70*

proximity prox-im´-i-ty noun closeness *60, 120*

prudence pru´-dence noun showing of good judgment *78*

public larder pub´-lic lar´-der noun place where the food for a town is stored *62*

put a damper on put a damp´-er on *phrase* made less; decreased *114*

quarter quar´-ter *noun* mercy given to a defeated enemy *135*

ration ra´-tion *noun* allowance of food for a day *63, 158, 168*

receptacles re-cep´-ta-cles *noun* containers or boxes *39*

reconnoitered rec-on-noi´-tered *verb* made an examination or took a survey of *172*

redcoats red´-coats *noun* British soldiers *13, 23, 33*

redoubts re-doubts´ *noun* low walls built outside a fortification to defend it *152, 157, 158*

reduction re-duc´-tion *noun* the conquering of *283*

refractory re-frac´-to-ry *adjective* stubborn; hard to manage *81*

rejoinder re-join´-der *noun* reply or answer *236*

remonstrate re-mon´-strate *verb* to plead or beg in protest *245*

rent rent *verb* tore; split *291*

report re-port´ *noun* a loud noise or explosion *53, 184*

reprimanded rep´-ri-mand-ed *verb* rebuked; corrected *77*

rheumatism rheu´-ma-tism *noun* pain in the joints and muscles *147*

rod rod *noun* a unit of measure equal to 16 1/2 feet *158, 183*

round round *noun* a single shot *167*

round price round price *noun* large or considerable price *64*

rout rout *verb* force out *227*

Royal Welsh Fusileers Roy´-al Welsh Fu-si-leers´ *noun* special division
of soldiers armed with a light flintlock musket *176*

ruse ruse *noun* trick *53, 96*

sally sal´-ly *noun* sudden rushing out to attack *148, 236*

sally port sal´-ly port *noun* opening through which soldiers would rush
out to fight *188*

sanctimonious sanc-ti-mo´-ni-ous *adjective* pretending to be holy or
pious *17*

sash sash *noun* wooden frame holding the glass in a window *27*

schooner schoon´-er *noun* ship with two or more masts *63, 70, 102*

scrutiny scru´-ti-ny *noun* careful examination *112*

secretary sec´-re-tar-y *noun* a writing desk, topped with a small
bookcase *18, 234*

secreted se-cret´-ed *verb* hidden *16*

see through the millstone see through the mill´-stone *phrase* solve
the riddle *105*

sepulchre sep´-ul-chre *noun* vault used for burial *229*

shades of night shades of night *noun* night shadows *161*

shindy shin´-dy *noun* noisy fight or row *157*

shoals shoals *verb* becomes shallow *91*

sixpence piece six´-pence piece *noun* coin worth six pence or half a shilling *41*

skirmish skir´-mish *noun* small battle *284*

skulking skulk´-ing *verb* moving in a stealthy or sneaky way *225*

sloops sloops *noun* ship with a single mast *63, 64, 66, 67*

smallpox small´-pox *noun* a serious disease that leaves people with scars or pocks when the disease is over *32, 297*

smock frock smock frock *noun* a loose shirt worn over the clothes to protect them *43*

souse souse *verb* put out by making wet *28*

square accounts square ac-counts´ *verb phrase* paying back; getting even *18*

stern sheets stern sheets *noun* the open spaces in the rear of a boat which don't contain seats *91*

stock stock *noun* handle or main part of a weapon, usually made of wood *46, 197*

stolen a march stol´-en a march *phrase* gained an advantage without being seen *164*

stupor stu´-por *noun* state of shock, in which the person appears to have lost the use of his senses *208*

suffice it to say suf-fice´ it to say *verb phrase* it is enough to say *16*

superfluous su-per´-flu-ous *adjective* more than what is wanted; excessive *216*

superseded su-per-sed´-ed *verb* replaced *283*

surmised sur-mised´ *verb* guessed or imagined *50, 78*

swivel gun swiv´-el gun *noun* mounted gun on a ship that can be aimed by moving it on its base *69, 93, 104*

taken time by the fore tak´-en time by the fore´-l *phrase* made good use of time *102*

taking off tak´-ing off *verb phrase* killing *162, 190*

tallow tal´-low *noun* animal fat used in candles *28, 30*

tantalized tan´-ta-lized *verb* teased *177*

taproom tap´-room *noun* barroom or tavern *241*

temperance tem´-per-ance *noun* not drinking liquor *245*

tethered teth´-ered *verb* tied to a long rope *145*

tidings tid´-ings *noun* news *60, 204*

timepiece time´-piece *noun* a watch *18*

tinder tin´-der *noun* any dry material that easily catches on fire *24, 233*

to bay to bay *verb* to be cornered with no escape or way out *269*

tocsin toc´-sin *noun* warning bell or signal *59*

token of submission to´-ken of sub-mis´-sion *noun* sign or symbol of giving up or surrendering *54*

Tory To´-ry *noun* a person who sided with the British in the American Revolution *17, 34, 35*

tried as with fire tried as with fire *verb* severely tested *207*

trying circumstances try´-ing cir-cum-stan´-ces *noun* difficult situations that severely test and strain people *54*

twitted twit´-ted *verb* teased; made fun of *126*

unceremoniously un-cer-e-mo´-ni-ous-ly *adverb* not in the usual way; not in a polite way *268*

unearthed un-earthed´ *verb* discovered *148*

unscrupulous un-scru´-pu-lous *adjective* without any idea of what is right and wrong *220*

village green vil´-lage green *noun* piece of land or park for common use in a village *61*

vindicate vin´-di-cate *verb* defend; protect from attack *13*

vouchsafed vouch-safed´ *verb* kindly or graciously given *79*

wardrobe ward´-robe *noun* a movable closet where clothes are stored *268*

whaleboats whale´-boats *noun* long, large rowboats, pointed at both ends *283*

Whigs Whigs *noun* people who supported the American Revolution *230, 236*

wicket wick´-et *noun* a small door set in a larger door *119*

without more ado with-out´ more a-do´ *phrase* with no more fuss or talk *37*

wrench wrench *verb* take away violently, by force *48*

zealous zeal´-ous *adjective* showing great dedication or enthusiasm *172*